TERMINAL ZONES

TERMINAL ZONES

GARETH E. REES

Influx Press
London

Published by Influx Press
The Greenhouse
49 Green Lanes, London, N16 9BU
www.influxpress.com / @InfluxPress
All rights reserved.
© Gareth E. Rees, 2022

First edition 2022. Printed and bound in the UK by TJ Books.

Paperback ISBN: 9781914391132
Ebook ISBN: 9781914391149

Editors: Gary Budden, Dan Coxon
Proofreader: Trudi Suzanne Shaw
Cover design: Vince Haig
Interior design: Vince Haig

CONTENTS

In memory of Hendrix (2008-2022)

My companion on many walks through
marshlands, coastlands, car parks and industrial
estates. Without him, these stories would not have
come into being.

WE ARE THE DISEASE

On a grey day, we set sail from Murmansk on the International Research Vessel *Salvo*, passing rows of container cranes and the hulks of decommissioned icebreakers, our worn-out predecessors, doomed to rust. We numbered seventy-five coastguard crew and forty-three scientists. For most on board, it was just another job, and we entered the Barents Sea on course for the Arctic Ocean with no great trepidation about what lay ahead. No sense of approaching disaster. Not of the unexpected kind, anyway. For we lived daily inside the slow catastrophe of the Great Warming. Dead reefs, mass extinctions and rising seas. Flooded cities. Wars over resources. You couldn't escape it. Every minor act – from switching on a light to flushing a toilet or munching on a loaf of bread – contributed to the crisis. Our very existence spelled the end of ourselves, so the notion that something might lie ahead on this voyage which was worse, and more terrifying, did not enter my mind, even though my role on the ship was to look out for imminent dangers.

I led a team which carried out inspections of the *Salvo*, checking for signs of fire or flood, so that the scientists had peace of mind to carry out their studies, which were of immense importance to the future of humankind. The ice caps were shrinking. Thinning sheets, like magnifying glasses, channelled the sun's rays into parts of the polar ocean that had been in lifeless darkness beneath thick ice for millions of years, before the rise and fall of civilisations. Light had woken the deep, microbial past. Vast blooms of algae flourished beneath the ice in creeping carpets of green and red. Scientists now believed that the levels of photosynthesis in the Arctic Ocean were ten times higher than previously thought. There was a glimmer of hope that this burgeoning bacterial life could help trap carbon dioxide from the atmosphere and slow the process of global warming. But there was also a larger fear that something novel was emerging which could further endanger human life, like those viral escapees from felled rainforests which had unleashed such devasting pandemics over the past decade. But we needed more data. So this was our purpose: to observe the largest possible extent of the bloom, at the tail end of the summer, before the sunlight vanished.

As with any voyage, we braced for violent, unpredictable weather. Savage storms. Freak waves. Big freezes could grip the pole at any time. Despite its thinning, the ice was not to be underestimated. Rather, instability made it more dangerous. It could close in fast. Entomb ships on gargantuan floes, powerless, like wildebeest in a tar pit. Many sailors became spooked. We'd heard recent reports from freighter ships of disturbances beneath the aurora borealis, geysers of light bursting from the ice, screams in the ether, incomprehensible voices, and impossible creatures glimpsed momentarily through blizzards, larger than the extinct polar bear. Of course, we were a scientific mission and didn't believe this literally. But we were well travelled on this ocean and understood their hysteria. The planet was in awful transformation. Its northern ice cap an expression of its death frenzy, flinging out wild magnetic tentacles as it dissolved into water. This was why we were heading there on the *Salvo*. To find out what was really going on.

In early August, we manoeuvred between sculpted icebergs of brilliant blue until we reached the pack ice, where the *Salvo* forced its way through narrow channels between jagged white plains, dotted with emerald pools. There was a dirty, grubby greenness to the outer rims of the ice where it met the water, as if it was rotting from beneath. We moored for a week at a time, while a team led by Chung and Pokrovsky took samples and brought them onto the ship for the biologists to work on. At mealtime presentations, they shared their findings. The bloom was spreading towards the pole, further north than ever recorded, a hundred and fifty miles of the stuff. The sixth mass global extinction counterbalanced by this subaquatic arctic rebirthing.

'Far more production is happening under the ice than we realised,' Chung announced one day in the canteen, 'and the algae is not behaving in the way we expected. It has evolved weird genetic mutations that make it… hard to classify… it will take time for us to make sense of it.'

On afternoons off, crew members played football in arctic gear on snow-dusted ice and returned with white eyebrows. My cabinmate, Svenson, was always urging me to play, but I preferred to take in views of the constantly mutating icescape, draw sketches in my notebook and idle with my daydreams. This was why I'd taken on this job, to leave the city and experience the world, to have space to think and breathe. I was in thrall to the possibilities of the moment, the beauty of the now. Gazing at the crystal vista beneath the endless sky, I could forget about droughts and forest fires, riots and famines, nuclear bomb tests and the epidemic of super-immune bacteria that had killed my parents, encouraging my attempt to escape from it all through a job on a research vessel. Missions like ours and those in the depths of the Marianas Trench were, in part, an attempt to find new antibiotics and genetic solutions in the bodies of undiscovered oceanic life forms. Science was a desperate affair these days. I felt sorry for the experts on board, clutching at straws, but this was paid work and it was good to be out in Earth's last clean air.

In late September, we cut deeper north, crunching through white slabs, meringue pieces crushed by the knife of the *Salvo*'s bow. Freezing winds made external work painful as the sun dropped ever lower and daytime became a persistent twilight. Days before we were due to turn back for port, we received a distress signal from the American container ship *Witness*, which had become trapped in pack ice. We were the only icebreaker with any chance of reaching it. The trip took four days through insane weather. A storm blackened the stars and trembled the masts. Strange phosphorescent green light shimmered around the hull of the *Salvo* as it bucked and heaved. A problem with the satellite communication forced us to broadcast on crackly old radio frequencies. Messages from the *Witness* grew garbled, fuzzy, then died out completely. Eventually, thick blizzard revealed an enormous dark shape like a tilted tower block. It was the *Witness*. We pushed through to get as close as we could. There were no lights. No sign of life. For all it appeared, the ship was abandoned decades ago.

A brief lull in the storm the following morning allowed Davydkin to take a rescue team across the ice, bowed into the wind, calling urgently through a loudhailer. Hours later, they returned, pale and shaken. The container ship was deserted, its floors coated in slippery algae and fungal growth on the walls. Much of the furniture was littered with tiny white flakes and gossamer-thin sheets of unidentified matter. They brought samples for Chung and Pokrovsky's team to analyse. We were all unnerved but Svensen and I dutifully continued our rounds of inspection, along with Wilkinson, our third team member, who seemed particularly on edge. Eventually, she told us with some embarrassment that it felt as if there was a fourth person with us. She couldn't explain why. Svensen remarked that the same thing happened to Ernest Shackleton and his companions as they made a desperate walk to Stromness, a whaling station in South Georgia, to get help for their stricken exploration party. I knew of that tale too, but I didn't feel a presence so much as a dread that something terrible was happening which we did not understand.

That night the gales returned with force, rattling our ship to its bones, howling through the vents as the ice pressed in hard against the hull. The captain sent out an SOS, although nobody could reach us, not in this storm, not this far north. On the third day, the radio died and our ship lost all communications. But for the American container ship concealed behind the whirling blizzard, we were alone at the end of the world. With horror, it dawned on me that I was stuck on a vessel embedded in an ice floe on a planet in the gravitational grip of a sun that turned in the Milky Way within a universe held together by dark matter. I was trapped. We all were. And we always had been. As I looked out at the ice floe, I felt nausea at the sudden awareness that I was glued to an incomprehensibly large and unknowable object, like a gnat stuck to a tractor wheel. It moved regardless of me, unheeding of my feelings. Unaware, even, of my existence.

To try and take my mind off things, I played poker with Svenson and Wilkinson in the recreation room, but we couldn't relax. Not when we heard rumours regarding the latest discovery in the lab. Those mysterious deposits found on the container ship were undoubtedly, irrefutably, almost certainly – it was said in hushed gasps - *human skin*. The captain assured us that as soon as the storm passed we would cut our way free and return home. But this directive was soon to change. New calls of alarm rippled through the *Salvo* when it became evident that someone was on board the trapped American container ship, after all. We could see it with our own eyes through the spiralling snowflakes. Lights beamed from the tilted deck of the *Witness*. It was astonishing. Some crew members claimed they saw shadows flit in the windows. We speculated that the crew, or whatever was left of it, had been in hiding from our rescue team when they boarded earlier. But why?

It took another day for the weather to give us a second chance to cross the ice to inspect the stricken vessel. Nervously, I watched Davydkin's team file across the snowdrifts until they disappeared into the murk. When they didn't return within twenty-four hours, a second party went out to investigate. They didn't come back either. The only thing that returned was a second storm which obliterated our view of the *Witness* and trapped us inside our own vessel, shaken by booms of thunder, the likes of which I'd never heard at sea.

The captain held an emergency briefing with his highest-ranking officers while the rest of us tried to carry on with our work. But panic had turned the mood. There was palpable tension in the canteen. At dinner, the usually level-headed Pokrovsky, leader of the biological analysis team, unleashed an extraordinary outburst. He clawed at his own cheeks and neck. Shrieked something about it getting under his skin. When Chung tried to calm him down, he flung himself upon her, biting and scratching. It took three crew members to drag him off her and confine him to his cabin. As an emergency measure, it was decided that the scientists should relax for the night. Down tools. Read in bed. Watch some movies. In the morning the captain would announce a plan. In the meantime, my team would continue our rounds as usual, ensuring the ship was safe.

Inside the *Salvo*, all was well, structurally speaking, despite the battering winds and shifting pack ice. Svensen, Wilkinson and I found nothing amiss. But it was when we braved the deck that we saw something out on the ice, a darkness against the white, expanding and shrinking like a lung. Through binoculars I could make out a giant, slug-like shape. A walrus, suggested Svenson, but it couldn't be. This had no discernible mouth, flippers, nor any consistency to its size and shape as it writhed slowly closer. I assigned a nightwatchman to keep track in case it tried to breach the hull, but he told us the next morning that the beast had seemingly plunged directly down into the ice. That was impossible, but we could see in the murky daylight that it had gone, leaving only a long, meandering red strip, marking its movement. Blood, we thought. Perhaps it was a walrus after all, wounded by our bow.

Wilkinson and I braved the gale to go onto the ice and check. 'This isn't blood,' said Wilkinson, dabbing and sniffing at the red smear, 'this is something else.' We hacked away a chunk and took it back to the ship for the biologists to test. But the lab was locked. Chung, deeply affected by the missing rescue teams and Pokrovsky's attack the previous evening, had suffered a breakdown, we were told. Crying, wailing, ranting about pain in her skin. She too had been confined to a cabin. As had several more of their team, all in states of distress, marked by outbursts of vitriol and violence. Others, including coastguard crew, lined up to see the doctor, complaining of rashes, nausea, stomach ache. Scuffles broke out in the corridor as they grew impatient and aggressive. We could only find one scientist willing to look at our hunk of stained ice. He had no doubt about what the red substance was.

'Spores,' he said, scratching his arms. 'Those are spores.'

It was hard to know what to do for the best. There were not enough remaining coastguard crew who were in the right state of mind to deal with the escalating situation. The labs had shut down. There were no scientists left to talk to. Nobody was interested in finding the cause of our woes. It was enough effort simply to keep order from breaking down entirely.

At breakfast the next morning, Wilkinson solemnly showed me her fingernails. They were green with fungal growth. Her toes too. Everything itched. She had this urge, she said, to leap out onto the ice to freeze it off, to cleanse herself. I told her to stay calm, see the doctor immediately, get some treatment for the disease now while she could. At this her face soured. She let out a scream, grabbed a fork like a dagger and came at me across the table, her teeth bared. 'It's you,' she said, 'you're the disease.' Two crewmen grabbed her and dragged her kicking to her quarters, where they locked her inside.

Svenson and I did our rounds that day without Wilkinson, trying to ignore the clamour of distressed voices echoing down the corridors, as the incarcerated rattled the doors of their locked quarters and cried out for release.

'We are thirsty for light!' pleaded Pokrovsky.

'The itch,' screamed Chung, 'it's unbearable. Take it off. Let me out of it!'

It was so sad that Wilkinson had been infected by the malady spreading through the *Salvo*. The signs were there, I supposed, when she'd told us the other day of her uneasy feeling that we were being stalked by invisible entities. Svenson shook his head. 'I don't know about you,' he said, 'but I have this eerie feeling that someone else is here with us. A presence. Can you not feel it?'

'Feel what?' I said.

'As if we are more than what we are.' Svenson frowned, seemingly confused by his own words. 'That we are legion.'

'Oh God, not you too.'

When we reached the bridge to report to the captain, we found him alone, staring out over the ice, a tumbler of whisky in his hand. More of the crew had succumbed, he told us, to whatever it was – mass hysteria or infectious disease, he knew not which. It had been the scientists, mainly, at first. But now his deck officer and chief engineer had gone stark raving mad. As soon as this storm abated, the captain promised, we'd leave this place.

But what kind of place was this? I wondered. It was a block of ice moving in a body of water on a spinning globe in the blackness of space. What place were we thinking of leaving? And where, precisely, were we planning to flee? There was nothing but the world and we were inescapably of that world. It was outside and inside us. Microbes thrived in our bodies, digesting our food, defending our immune systems, transmitting signals to our brains. They were in the sea. On the land. In our cities. In our water supply. Beneath the ice of the Arctic, blooming and mutating, seeping up into the light. There was nowhere to go but here, and here was everywhere.

That night, Svenson woke me up as he clattered down from his bunk, furiously scratching his stomach. 'I need to see Wilkinson,' he muttered, swiftly exiting in only his T-shirt and underpants. Groggy from sleep, I became aware of a commotion outside. Yelling and screaming. The slam of doors. I pulled on some clothes and a jacket and left the cabin. A terrified Russian cook ran past me. 'They're out,' he yelled. 'They're getting out.'

I hurried after him as he hurtled down the steps, into the kitchen where there were staff huddled together by the ovens, clutching an array of sharp implements. The situation had escalated, it seemed. So many crew members had become gripped by the madness that it became impossible for those who remained sane to contain them. Now the infected were opening the doors of locked cabins, letting people out, and all hell had broken loose. Some were even escaping from the ship and heading onto the ice, heedless of the wind and snow, to face their certain deaths.

Wilkinson. I had to find Wilkinson.

Grabbing a long knife from the rack, I left the kitchen and made my way through the ship in search of her, hiding from the occasional crew member as they hurtled past in the grip of their mania, half-dressed or even naked. I checked in the empty cabins of the infected to see psoriatic flakes of skin piled on the furniture and the bedding shredded. As I feared, Wilkinson wasn't in her quarters. There were smears of blood on her sheets and something scratched into the metal of her bunk in a spidery scrawl:

WE ARE THE DISEASE

As I headed to the main deck, I spotted Svenson in his underwear, running up some stairs, his screams less those of pain and more a kind of war cry. I called out his name and he turned briefly, eyes wild, then sprang from view. I hurried after him onto the deck but he had vanished. It was hard to make out anything clearly in a darkness obfuscated by snow, but in the shimmering lights of the *Salvo* I saw a figure below. It was Wilkinson, or the top half of her, anyway, embedded in the ice, clad only in a T-shirt. She steadily and rhythmically paddled her arms as if wading, waist deep, against fast-moving water. Luminescent algae streamed up through the cracks in the surface around her midriff, turning her exposed arms and neck green, illuminating her face, stricken with a combination of terror and ecstasy.

'Wilkinson!' I cried out. 'Ellen!'

I thought for a moment she could hear me. Her head tilted at an angle, mouth opening as if to speak, and out poured a column of black, viscous matter. It kept coming and coming, thickening into a black coil around her torso, expanding and contracting. Breathing. I staggered back with a cry. Behind me there was a loud click as the door opened and the captain emerged, uniform in shreds, shocked momentarily by the blast of wind, looking frantically around him as if for an escape. I raised my quivering knife in defence, and he came rushing at me in a fury, then flipped over the edge. I didn't peer down to see what happened to him, because other figures on deck were moving erratically in my direction, barking nonsensical gibberish. I lost my nerve and I fled.

We cannot stop them. All that we thirteen remaining, uninfected crew members can do is barricade ourselves into the kitchens, where there are supplies of food and knives behind heavy doors. Here we must wait out the storm. At night, the ice pushes so hard against us it feels as if the ship will split and take us down into the infested depths. Despite the gale howling through the vents and rattling the gantry we can hear them, the sluggish entities that crawl up the hull and seethe on the upper decks, releasing spores into the wind. They drone and weep and seep their strange microbial cacophony into my thoughts. Even when I put my fingers in my ears, the noise roars within me, through the rivers of my blood, in the forests of my gut flora, across the teeming oceans inside my cells. The sound is outside and inside and nothing makes a difference. It will never go away. It feels like there's a coating of slime on my skin. I cannot see it, but I know it is there. I have the urge to tear it off, rip myself out of myself, become something other, something not of this world, of this universe, this waking nightmare. But I don't tell the others. If they find out, they may kill me or eject me from the ship.

As a last resort, I have taken to scribing this private journal of events, which, I suspect, will be the only evidence left on board the *Salvo* of what has occurred. A written legacy left to whatever remains of humanity, for as long as it lasts. Our only hope is that we thirteen are somehow immune, that the gales die down and we can steer this ship free with a skeleton crew. In that unlikely event, we will have to abandon our friends and colleagues on this frozen plateau, to the mercy of the algae bloom, and to each other. In the darkest hours, we can hear them outside, whooping and screaming, hurling obscenities at the stars, and we are so afraid.

WHEN NATURE CALLS

Maleeka opened the back door of their bungalow to discover that their water butt had vanished. The vegetable patch was still there. The electricity generator and greenhouse, too – just about – but where the butt had been was now thin air. Carefully, she dropped to her knees and crawled to the cliff edge. On the shore, thirty metres below, the big green container poked from a pile of rubble, topped with bits of lawn. It was getting dark. Dirty clouds amassed over an English Channel that was rising quickly, drowning rocks and turning the sandstone blood-red. Tonight's full moon meant the tide would be extra high. After a week of heavy rain, who knew what else they might lose before the morning?

She returned to the kitchen to tell Rizzie. At the news, Rizzie suddenly looked much older than her sixty-seven years. 'Have we any water bottles left?'

'I filled one earlier,' said Maleeka.

'Then we can have a cuppa, at least.' Rizzie opened the cupboard above the kettle and stared into it for a while. Finally, she said, 'Where's the tea?'

'I think we finished it.'

Rizzie sighed. 'Then there's nothing to be done. Nothing.'

'You should have said.'

'It's always me, ain't it? I should have said, I should have said. What about you? What should *you* have said? You always wait till the last moment, right until the point when things run out. Then suddenly you pipe up. You're a late piper, that's what you are.'

'That's not true.'

'When I think of all these years you've been living here…'

There was a knock at the door.

'Shit on a stick, this is all we need,' said Rizzie, hobbling arthritically into the living room. 'If that's Brian – and I can't think who else it could possibly be – then let's kill him and steal his tea. We've sod all to lose.'

* * *

Rizzie's parents named her Elizabeth, which she hated, but rarely heard it said from their lips. Her mum was an addict who bed-hopped through the back streets of Brighton, while dad was nothing more than a series of letters sent from oil rigs where he worked before he started a new family somewhere in Scotland. She was brought up in Hastings by

Granny Stamford, or Peg as she insisted on being called. Peg was a fiercely funny armchair raconteur surrounded by books on almost every subject, from mechanical engineering and black magic to medieval poetry and archaeology. She told Rizzie that thirteen thousand years ago, long before the pyramids, there was a matriarchal moon-worshipping civilisation with an intricate knowledge of the stars, electricity and engineering. It thrived until a comet hit the Earth, melting the North American ice sheet and causing a great flood that destroyed almost every trace of that civilisation. Men had since thrived on our amnesia.

Peg's feminist pseudohistories pleased Rizzie as a goth teenager in the late eighties, skinning up for the skinny lads beneath the pier, which is how she earned her nickname. As soon as she was able, she left for London to seek emancipation. By 1993 she lived in a Leyton squat, protesting the M11 link road, a monstrous tarmac river spilling through the middle of an East London community, demolishing everything in its path. Claremont Road was the last bastion of defence, a Victorian street blocking the capitalist highway. They offered tenants cash incentives for abandoning their properties. Then they sent in bailiffs, riot cops and dogs to force out the rest. She lived for months under siege, behind boarded doors, sun slanting through the gaps, listening to protestors and police bark at each other through megaphones. The pigs won, of course, as they always did. The walls torn away even as they huddled within. Houses pulled down, the new road built, and cars whizzing through the ghost of a community as if nothing had happened.

Things were never the same after that. Rizzie endured a succession of clerical office jobs that paid for enough cider at the weekend to stay hungover from Monday to Friday, when she could do it all over again. A decade passed like this before she returned to Hastings, where she tried to avoid her youthful haunts and bad-penny lovers who turned up on her doorstep. Fortunately, her dad died just after her thirty-sixth birthday and left her nineteen grand in his will. Guilt money, she presumed. It was enough to get a bungalow in Fairlight a few streets back from the cliff edge, where she could see the sea from the garden if she stood on a bucket and peered through a gap in the houses on Sea Road. On the first day, a stray cat wandered into the house and curled up on the rug. In that instant, Rizzie knew she would never call another place home.

That was almost thirty years and god knows how many cats ago. Rizzie was now the age Granny Stamford was when she died. Sea Road had since dropped into the sea, leaving her bungalow with a front row seat. She could open the door and look out over the English Channel with its storm clouds and container ships, and see the helicopters buzz to Dungeness or industrial rescue vessels pump showers of rock onto the shingle around the troubled power station. Some days, hot sun beat on her greenhouse full of organic vegetables and marijuana plants. But more often, monsoon rains nourished her potatoes and leeks. On balmy evenings she sat with her cats, listening to the hum of the generator, blowing smoke rings and drinking tea, a pleasure now lost because half her garden was at the bottom of the cliff along with a week's worth of collected rain water, and the bloody Syrian had forgotten to get teabags.

To make things worse, here was Brian on the doorstep. Busybody twat-in-a-mac Brian with a bundle of papers in his hands. Behind him the first dots of rain fell on cracked pavements broken by buddleia and thistle. He didn't wait for Rizzie's invitation and shuffled into the living room where Maleeka was lighting candles. Rizzie was certain that Maleeka was the sole reason he remained in Fairlight. The rest of the village had taken the compensation money and run – 'managed retreat', the government called it. Bloody sell-outs. Rizzie believed it was immoral to take money for abandoning the home she loved. She'd been through this before in Leyton in '94. They'd said she was a fool, but if you don't live by your principles, you might as well throw yourself into the ocean anyway.

'I brought something for ya to look at.' Brian thudded the papers on the coffee table, frightening a cat from under it. 'I know you ladies have something against the internet… and TVs… and phones… so I took the liberty…'

'Ha! That's bang on,' snapped Rizzie, closing the door. 'Liberties, Brian. We all got 'em, but some people want to take 'em from us. Ain't that right, Leeka?'

'Very good,' said Brian. 'Thing is, see, Maleeka, I wanted to show you the latest predictions. These are fresh from the government website… coastal management 2037… moving forward to 2047.' He held up a piece of paper with map of Fairlight on it. 'We are standing, right now, all of us, above what is going to be a bay in less than a year… a *bay*, do you hear? The cliff won't hold. You can't stop the water.'

'Why do you assume I think water can be stopped?' said Maleeka. 'You think I don't know about water?'

'Well, y'know…' Brian blushed and looked down at his feet. 'I'm sorry, Maleeka.'

Maleeka's two children floating face down in the Aegean beside an upturned boat. That's what all three of them saw that moment, as hard rain began to fall, hammering the roof. Rizzie had found Maleeka on the streets of Hastings a year after she made it to Britain from Syria, shivering with cold. She gave her sanctuary in Fairlight where she taught her to tend the vegetable garden, feed chickens, fix the generator, swear like a trooper, and live a life off-grid. No governments, no pesticides, no fluoride, no internet, no television, and no need for men. They got everything they could want from a marriage – all the collaboration, company and bickering – without the sex and physical combat. This was what made Brian so irritating, lingering in their living room with his dyed comb-over and meaty odour.

'I want to help,' he said, reaching for Maleeka's hand. She didn't take it. 'You don't understand the danger. Come to my place, stay a while and we'll make a plan.' He turned to Rizzie, his smile crooked. 'Of course, I – I – I mean the both of you.'

'We have five cats,' said Rizzie. 'They'll tell us when we need to move out. They can sense danger, cats. Famous for it.'

'When you see what I printed out, you'll change your tune. Just give me a chance.' Brian pointed to the hallway. 'But first can I use yer loo?' He shambled down the hall and shut the toilet door with a soft click.

'What if he's right, Rizzie?' whispered Maleeka.

'Don't start.'

'Maybe it's inevitable.'

'We got years left, years I tell ya. They're all scaremongers.'

'But when it comes…'

'*If* it comes.'

'Sorry, Rizzie, but I believe that what's happening is the will of—'

'Don't say it, Leeka. Don't invoke his name. He who does not exist.'

Maleeka didn't know much about what was happening to the ice caps and the weather but she had never lost her faith, despite all she had suffered. It was every good Muslim's duty to nurture the earth, and she had done so to the best of her ability. But perhaps the time had come to leave their garden. Long ago, the Arabian Peninsula had been a verdant meadowland. It was narrated in a hadith that the Messenger of Allah declared 'the Hour will not begin until the land of the Arabs once again becomes meadows and rivers'. Now the rains were returning like the prophesy said. England's suffering was not her homeland's. It might be that this was the will of Allah. Perhaps the return of the meadows would bring peace to the Middle East and she could return home from exile, taking Rizzie with her.

'You're as bad as those wizards,' said Rizzie, settling into her armchair, kicking Brian's papers onto the floor so she could rest her feet on the table.

'This is different.'

'No it ain't, you all think something better's coming and you wanna cheer it on, waving your little flags.'

Maleeka remembered the wizards well enough. Not long after Sea Road collapsed and the government announced the coastal roll-back, men in black robes and tall black hats began to appear on the shore. Sharing a joint in their deck chairs at the edge of the garden, Maleeka and Rizzie watched in amusement as the men arranged coloured stones in circles and danced around fires, flicking water from buckets. A few weeks later a different group appeared, this time men in white robes and white hats. They set up further along the shore, using a similar combination of fire, water and stone. Every so often, a white-robed man in a pointed hat went to the water's edge and flung forward his arms as if to hurl them at the horizon. At this, a member of the black-robed group went over to remonstrate, jabbing a finger angrily at the man in the white pointed hat. The man in the white pointed hat jabbed back. At which point the black-hatted man knocked the white-hatted man's hat right off. A scuffle broke out, punches flying, men chasing each other up and down the foreshore, pulling each other's cowls over their heads and throwing stones. It seemed to go on for hours. The next afternoon, a group of black-robed men knocked at the door and explained that they were from an organisation called the OTO – the Ordo Templi Orientis.

'I know very well who you lot are,' Rizzie said. 'Crowley's black magic lot. My grandmother met your most famous member over in Hastings almost a century ago. He was a right cunt, apparently.'

'My apologies,' said a man with a black eye and a torn black hat under his arm. 'But Aleister Crowley was the gatekeeper of the apocalypse and finally the Aeon of Horus is upon us. Our work is urgent. I wonder if we might use your garden for a ceremony, free from disturbance by… certain undesirables.'

Rizzie's heart swelled with Granny Stamford's spirit. She couldn't stop herself. She just let fly.

'What is it about you men and the apocalypse? Does it get you hard or something? Hell's bloody bells! There *is* no apocalypse, there's only things growing and things dying and things growing again. It's how it was before us and how it'll be after we're gone. If you ever stopped to *smell the fucking flowers,* you'd understand. Now jog on.' She slammed the door.

After a few months, the beach became too dangerous for ceremonies, and the wizards went elsewhere. The last of Fairlight's residents packed their bags and left too. Nobody had been to their door in years. Except for Brian, of course. There was always Brian.

'What the hell is he doing in there anyway?' said Rizzie staring angrily towards the toilet. 'He's been an age.'

They sat for a while, listening to the cacophony of rain and wind. Candle flames guttered as waves crashed against the cliff. A rumble of thunder, like nothing they'd ever heard before, shook the house, smashed the glasses in their cupboards and sent trinkets flying from shelves. The women jumped from their chairs in fright. What a racket! Their frantic cats paced the room, mewing loudly. Yet still no Brian.

Tentatively, Maleeka went into the hall and called out, 'Brian? Are you alright in there, Brian? ...*Brian?'*

No reply.

'Call him "lover" or "darling",' said Rizzie, 'that'll do it. He'll come leaping out. You watch. Leaping out like the pranny he is.'

Maleeka giggled. 'Brian, *darling!'*

Another rumble of thunder.

'Oh for pity's sake.' Rizzie hobbled past Maleeka and shook the handle, but the door was locked. She rapped on the wood. 'Open up, Brian! Open up, you swine!'

'There must be something wrong,' said Maleeka. 'I'll give it a kick.'

'You what?'

31

'Like this.' Maleeka raised a foot and slammed it hard into the door. It swung open to reveal a universe in collapse. A mass of sulphurous cloud swirled towards the moon in a roar of noise, as if the world was being sucked through a vent in space. The English Channel was a seething tumult, the waves an infinity of shark fins racing inland. With a cry, they held onto each other tight, bracing themselves in the doorway to oblivion. At their feet was a sheer drop to a sea fizzing with acid rain. The entire back wall and floor of the toilet were gone. Only the side walls remained, jutting out over the cliff. The toilet roll, still in its holder, was unspooled all the way down, a ribbon of white paper dangling into the blackness like the world's worst bungee cord. Brian was about to wipe when the floor gave way, and held on to the paper until the very end. Below them, water exploded against rock. Chunks of wood and plaster spun in phosphorescent foam. But no sign of Brian. He was gone.

'Well, that's the end of that,' muttered Rizzie. She felt nothing but a hole where her heart had been.

'Brian!' Maleeka cried into the rain. 'Brian, I'm sorry!' Twenty years fell away and an ocean of pain rushed in. 'My children, my children, my children…'

For a moment, they stared into the sea which had taken their generator, their greenhouse, their toilet, their neighbour, and turned them to flotsam. Then they fled to the living room, where their terrified cats scratched at the porch door. They grabbed their coats. There was no need for keys. Not any more. It was time to go. Rizzie knew that now. You can ignore the prophets, the politicians and all the Brians. But when nature calls, everyone must run.

A DREAM LIFE OF HACKNEY MARSHES

1. THE BIG BANG

There was a time before I fell in love with a pylon on Hackney Marshes.

Back then, I lived with my girlfriend Ruth in a converted clothes factory in Dalston. I was doing okay writing radio ads, brochures and guidebooks. I was sent cheques. I laughed on a wobbly bicycle all the way to the bank. We drank the profits and partied all weekend.

One summer day, I got married to Ruth in a black lamé suit and a cowboy hat. She wore a pretty dress. The sun blazed. A psych-rock band played. We got on a plane to Colombia. The party moved to South America. Bingo bango bosh. Life was still okay.

Then we came back, and everything changed.

We bought our own place, the way grownups do. A small flat in Clapton. On the day after we moved in, Ruth discovered she was pregnant. She gave up the drink and I cut down. There were no more parties. I started to watch Saturday night television. For the first time in my life, I bought a lawnmower. I listened to Radio 4. There was an apple tree in our garden. How strange, I thought, to own a source of fruit.

When I stepped off the hedonistic treadmill, everything began to ache. My back, my knee, my wrists, my bones. Pain flashed through my fingers when I typed. Sure signs of repetitive strain injury. I spent hours in quiet despair, eating cheese and thinking about death. Soon I grew a big fat Buddha belly.

A physiotherapist told me to spend less time at the computer, lose weight and do more exercise. I ignored her. Another physiotherapist told me the same.

'Just cure my pain,' I said. 'Please.'

No more help was forthcoming. So I tried acupuncture. I tried Pilates. I went for a swim at the London Fields Lido. I did everything the experts recommended. Nothing worked.

As a last resort I bought a dog. I'd always wanted one, but worried about being tied down. Now I was tied down alright. Strapped to the earth by legions of shrieking responsibilities. The foetus was growing. My wife was vomiting. There was a living room to be painted and furniture to buy. House prices had crashed. And however painful my repetitive strain injury was, the mortgage needed to be paid. To pay it I needed to write more words. And to write, I needed a cure for my pain.

A dog would give me enforced breaks from writing and a dose of exercise. If things got too much with the baby, I had an excuse to flee the house.

Besides, what harm could a dog do?

2. DOG

Max came from a breeder in Essex. He was the last in the litter. By the time we got him home, I realised I'd never seen his eyes open. I bought a book called *Cocker Spaniels*. Inside was a picture of a nine-week-old puppy with bright eyes, glossy coat and long limbs.

I stared at the photo. I stared at Max. He looked like a drowned mole. Fluid oozed from his tear ducts. He had bandy legs and dandruff. He tumbled around the kitchen, leaking piss and bumping into his crate.

'Shall we take him back?' I asked Ruth.

'He's a living thing.' She caressed her bump. 'You can't just send him back.'

The vet told me Max had congenital cataracts. He prescribed steroid drops. The drug kept Max's pupils frozen wide so light could flow round his cataracts and feed his retinas with images.

As soon as he was vaccinated, I took him to Millfields Park. That was the point, after all. Me. The dog. Being out and about.

We made it to the bottom of the slope, where the park plunged into the Lea Navigation. Across the water a concrete peninsula littered with piles of rubble. Seagulls. Barbed wire. Ducks.

On either side of this peninsula were two park exits. A footbridge over the canal and a steel rampart beneath the Lea Bridge Road. Flowing through these vents was a stream of human traffic. Cyclists, runners, dog-walkers, wasters, jabbering loons, couples, spliff-toting teenagers, baseball-capped men on bikes yelling through megaphones at rowing boats.

I'd no idea where they were coming from. I'd never heard of the Lea Valley nature reserve. All I knew about Hackney marshes was that people played football there on Sundays.

Now I was curious.

As soon as Max was able to walk the distance, I crossed the Rubicon. I took a brief glance behind me at the neat Victorian terraces of Clapton where my wife and unborn baby dwelled. For a moment, I considered turning back. Then I passed beneath Lea Bridge Road, where a splash of graffiti read:

YOUR SAFETY, OUR THREAT

3. PYLON

Almost immediately, I realised this was not London any more.

Max and I were on a towpath. Narrowboats lined the navigation, bedecked with pot plants and armchairs.

Smoke puffed from their tiny chimneys. A man sawed through a stack of wood. Geese bobbed on the water among Coke bottles and foam.

Set in a long red-brick wall were some iron gates. I entered and found myself on the ruins of a Victorian water filtration plant. Concrete pathways rose from circular beds. Service ladders disappeared into pools of rushes. Fragments of machinery jutted from the ramparts. I ran my hands over defunct cogs and the skeletons of pulley systems. In the centre of it all, a stone circle like a sundial where I spun slowly, amazed.

In one of the filter beds, giant ceramic fish heads and tails rose from the rushes. A weir rammed with nappies, cans and footballs gushed water into a river. Cormorants perched on rocks, preening themselves like creatures freshly dragged from an oil slick. A parakeet darted from a tree. Max sniffed at the remains of a sandwich. The air smelled of rotten leaves and bus fumes.

I wondered how such a place could exist on my doorstep. It didn't even feel like a place, but a space in between. A giant crack in the city where the detritus of London collected.

And then I saw her. Lurching from the scrub like a catwalk model, crackling with power and energy. My head told me it was just another electricity pylon but it was – *she* was – different. I couldn't take my eyes off her.

That's how it began.

The affair. If that's what you want to call it.

Like most of my relationships, it started slowly. Max and I walked by her slender steel body every day. But we didn't really connect. Not properly. It still hurts me to think of it. But it's true.

At first, too many other things caught my roving eye.

The abandoned toy factory, brooding by the navigation, windows smashed, loading hook like a torture instrument in the bay. Walthamstow Marsh where long-horned cattle grazed, framed by the silhouettes of City skyscrapers. The vast green sheet of the playing fields, stapled with goalposts, scuffed and scarred by a million Sunday League matches.

What was known as 'the marsh' was, I discovered, a string of marshes, building yards, bird sanctuaries, reservoirs, railway lines and underpasses. You could get lost in there. Wander into cul-de-sacs littered with fox shit, beer cans and wild flowers. Spend hours among mysterious concrete obelisks. Read graffiti arguments between cyclists, walkers, gangsters and artists. Listen to rats forage in the nettles. Stare down pipes into the bowels of the city. Hear the gurgle of subterranean rivers.

Each day I pushed further down a corridor of electricity pylons stretching from the edgelands of the A12, along the Eurostar lines, to Springfield Marina and the grand Victoriana of Stamford Hill.

I found the pylons magnificent but predictable. Each one led to the next in an endless parade. These giants were wedded to each other with loops of glass and cable. Manacled like slaves. Forced into enclaves of inaccessible scrub. Outcasts in a world that wished they weren't there, spoiling the view.

She was the exception. Indignant and inconvenient, she stood right there in the Middlesex filter beds, overlooking the art installations, tourist information boards and artificial ponds.

My pylon.

She'd been here all the time, waiting for me to notice her properly.

Funny how that happens in life. In love.

4. BIRTH

From the first day Sophia was born she puked. She shat. She screamed with colic. It was the end of sleep for Ruth and me. The end of sex, the end of meaningful conversation, and – for me – the end of writing.

For the first month, I dutifully followed the pair around, bunching nappies into balls, emptying bins. Did what dads were supposed to do. I hung about in doorways like a demented waiter with a muslin cloth draped over my arm.

'What does she want now?' I said, annoyed that I had to raise my voice over the caterwauling.

'She's hungry,' Ruth said.

'Sorry?'

'SHE IS HUNGRY.'

'What do you want me to do?'

'Nothing, as usual.' Ruth unbuttoned the breast-flaps of her maternity dress.

Christ. There was absolutely nothing good about this.

My wife was confined to the bedroom once again. She spent the days and nights in front of rolling property programmes, feeding like a sow, trying to keep the baby happy. She was fraught with worry. The relentless screaming, it was unnatural. Sophia clung to her with translucent fingers. If I tried to hold her, she'd writhe in my arms until I spilled her back onto Ruth's chest.

I bought a glossy hardback book called *Baby* by Desmond Morris. Inside were pictures of pink and peaceful newborn babies.

I stared at the photos. I stared at Sophia. She looked like a stricken bat. Her excrement smelled of sulphur. Ruth would point at the oily green spatter and say, 'Does that look normal to you?' I had no idea. It wasn't in the Desmond Morris book. I sat in grim silence next to the bed, handing out wet wipes, thinking of my next excuse to leave the room.

If I could manage an escape, I'd catch a little sleep on a rug beneath my desk. Max was usually there, curled up, oblivious. I seethed with envy for the dog's life. It was the only emotion I felt, in truth, but I didn't tell Ruth.

The pylon, though: she'd understand. That much I knew.

I thought my return to work would solve my problems. But the noise was more excruciating than the shooting pains in my arms. Sometimes I'd hear Ruth crying, too. I'd turn up the music in my office but it didn't mask the knowledge that they were next door, imploding.

At times I sensed Ruth standing in the doorway of my office behind me, holding our sick, yellow baby. I daren't turn round. Instead I'd hammer gibberish into my computer, as if rapt with inspiration, until she went away. Then I'd kill the words with the delete button.

A health screening company had commissioned me to write a mail order brochure for them. They wanted old people to get checked for their stroke and heart attack risk.

After two weeks I came up with a single headline:

IS YOUR LIFE OVER?

I spent many hours changing the font and text size. Large, small. Ariel. Helvetica. Garamond. Dingbats. Green, then red, then black, highlighted, underlined, in bold.

Then I deleted it and wrote:

READ THIS OR DIE

I blamed the tiredness. But I knew that it wasn't that. Not entirely.

That pylon, she was constantly at the back of my mind. A needle probing at the skin of every thought.

5. VISION

In rare moments when the house was quiet, I lay face down and sucked air through the gaps in the floorboards. I imagined the micro-world an inch beneath. The lice, the mites, locked in a battle for survival, hunting for food, living a wild life. I imagined that I was her, my pylon, looking down on wretched mankind with benevolence and love. I imagined that she saw me staring back at her, and that she felt a deep longing.

To take my mind off things, I watched a lot of television. Programmes about fat people. About unhappy people. About people winning and losing competitions.

About people cooking. About people having babies. Always the babies.

The doctor refused to accept there was anything wrong with ours. 'They do cry, you know,' he said, letting out a great big belly laugh.

Ruth went crazy at him, demanding to see a specialist. Nurses led her into a back room and tried to talk her down, stop her weeping. Later I got a phone call from a counsellor enquiring about her postnatal depression.

'Fuck you,' I said, which didn't help. Now we were on a register.

After that, I found it was best not to talk at all. Not around Ruth, or nurses, or doctors. So I started to avoid the family altogether. Half-hour dog walks became hour-long walks. Two-hour walks. Sometimes I'd be gone a whole afternoon.

I felt more at home on the marsh, roaming among the London tribes. Tracksuit gangsters with bullmastiffs. Hasidic Jews in high black socks and shiny shoes. Vociferous Turks. Pram-pushing Poles. Bearded old men with yappy dogs. Anorak nerds, supping from flasks. Lovers in the long grass. Cyclists with their Lycra bulges. Rastas, hippies, City boys, construction workers, drunks.

It was like strolling through a collective dream. And it felt good, being outside myself.

But not good enough.

This is why, I think, I started taking my dog's cataract medicine.

The first occasion was a mistake. I rubbed my eyes shortly after administering the drops to Max. Forty minutes later I could feel my irises tear open. Light flooded my retina.

The room was submerged in a psychedelic haze, pierced by shards of silver. Like a vision.

For a few hours, it was too much. I had to crouch in the wardrobe. Even then, rays of light still penetrated somehow. When I held my hand to my face I realised I could see in the dark. My hand was glowing. It was pylon-shaped.

Ruth mistook my reasons for being in the wardrobe. She stood there with the crying baby, speaking through the door.

'Charlie, I know you're finding this hard. But I don't have the energy to worry about you. I can't deal with two babies.'

'I can't hear you,' I said.

'I said that I'm not sorry for you.'

'Sorry?'

'I – AM – NOT – FEELING – SORRY – FOR – YOU.'

I'd had enough. I knew where I had to be right now and it wasn't with Ruth. I stepped out of the wardrobe.

'Max needs a walk.'

Sporting a pair of sunglasses, I hurried Max to the bottom of Millfields Park. We turned right under the bridge, as usual, past the weir and over the footbridge, towards the Middlesex filter beds.

Even with shades on there was so much light hitting the backs of my eyeballs that the world was in whiteout. It felt like I was stumbling towards the pearly gates, towards God. I entered the filter beds and wobbled across the ramparts, pools of fire on either side of me.

I was so desperate to see her I almost broke into a run. But there was no need. She emerged from the dazzle, a slender giant, looking almost wet in the shimmering light, like Ursula Andress striding from the ocean. She cackled and crackled. Lines of black cord whipped from her arms to embrace me.

I went to her, heart pumping. Stood dead centre between her four legs and gazed up. I gasped at the interplay of lines. The poetry of infinity in her delicate spirals of steel. She fired sunbeams at me through her gaping geometry. I laughed in response. I marvelled at the essence of her, trembling with electricity. I touched her legs, each clad in a garter of barbed wire, thrilled at the thought of the volts running through her.

For a moment, I imagined her in a black leather miniskirt and I felt an enormous, surprising erection.

But I did nothing about it.

I didn't want to sully the moment.

6. LOVE

Her name was Angel.

You can laugh. You can mock. But go and tell the captain of a ship he's deluded when he calls her by name. Tell that to the mountaineer who loves, fears and respects the peak that could kill him.

To me she wasn't a thing that had been constructed. She was a being who had descended from above. We'd found each other and nothing else mattered. I stopped going to the marina. I grew bored of watching the wrecking balls dismantle the toy factory. Max no longer got to wade in the Lee River's mudbanks or gambol among the upturned shopping trolleys.

Now it was all about Angel. I planned my days around her.

In the morning, I'd help at home with the nappies, the bottles, the puke. All that stuff. Really threw myself into it with gusto, so Ruth wouldn't know something was up. Then I'd go to the kitchen and prepare sandwiches. Triangle ones.

Ruth found me in the kitchen once, carefully measuring the angle of the bread.

'You're making sandwiches.'

I took the cheese out of the wrapper.

'Blue cheese,' Ruth said. 'You hate blue cheese. You say it tastes of metal.'

I froze. Did she suspect something?

'Things change.'

'Whatever, Charlie.'

She shuffled back to her bedroom, closed the door.

I tessellated the triangles in a Tupperware box. Carefully placed the box inside a leather satchel. Then off to the marsh.

That summer a gang of hedonistic narrowboat folk had moored outside the filter bed entrance. They wore trilbies and leather jackets. They cracked open beers in the late morning and wiled away the hours on sofas smoking weed. They blared dub reggae from an old ghetto blaster. They laughed a lot.

I'd pass them every day. They'd nod. I'd smile back. It was a happy time. They brought a carnival feel to the place. Every day a celebration. Magical.

Sometimes I'd sit on the bench next to Angel and feel her hum, my legs jiggling in front of me. Max would chase his shadow, or sleep in the shade. When he was settled I'd dab cataract medicine into each eye, wait for my pupils to crank open, the irises to fire up, then out with the iPhone.

I'd started recording a series of electronic mixtapes. Drone. Minimalist techno. Really it wasn't my taste. It was hers. I was only interpreting the vibrations. Giving her what she wanted. She loved the glitch sound. Our favourite track was 'Test Pattern #1111' by Ryoji Ikeda, a Japanese sound artist.

Together we'd sing it: 'Chk chk chk chck chck – tsssssssssssssssssssssssst – tk tkt tk tk tkt kk – tsssssssssssssssssssss – tk tk tkt tk.'

Afterwards I'd go between her legs and point my camera upwards, let the sun fragment in her girders, spatter rays across my lens. Gently she'd tickle the nape of my neck with volts. It was wonderful.

'Chk chk chk - tsssssssssssssssssssssssst,' I would coo.

'Tk tk tk tk.'

A quick cigarette and I was off round the filter beds, taking pictures from every angle, let her slip in and out of view, play peek-a-boo behind the bushes.

Over the weeks my photo library built up nicely. I kept pictures of her on a secret file named 'Work'. In the first four months of her life, we'd taken almost no photographs of Sophia. Why would we? We'd barely left the house as a family. She was constantly in pain.

As for Ruth and me, the happy couple, there was nothing to photograph. We'd vanished from our own marriage. We slept in alternative shifts, passed by each other with a grunt.

In this respect, the cataract medicine was an inconvenient habit. The effects lasted up to twelve hours and made sleep difficult. My head ached all the time. Whisky helped a little. I made sure I always carried a hipflask.

Angel didn't approve of the drinking. The silent treatment; always a giveaway. But I reasoned that relationships were all about accepting the idiosyncrasies of others. Drinking was mine, being an electricity pylon was hers.

But they were good days, mostly. At dusk I'd return, happy, from the marsh to find my family slumped like refugees in front of a flickering television. Often Ruth would murmur something at me, 'I miss you,' or, 'I love you.' I couldn't make it out. Never replied. My head was always banging with pain. I'd slide straight under the duvet.

Then one night, Ruth wasn't in bed. She was sitting in the living room with a brown envelope, trembling.

'I opened this,' she said. 'It's from the bank.'

'Right.' The letter didn't surprise me. I'd not done a single day's useful work in almost five months. The money had entirely run out. Letters were piling up. Bills. Overdrawn warnings. Council tax. Threats. I'd taken to stuffing them behind the filing cabinet so Ruth wouldn't see.

'But all that work you're doing on the computer...'

Electronic music mixtapes, arranging photos. These took time. Especially when your eyes were fucked. She'd never understand.

'It's all in hand,' I promised.

'Charlie.' Ruth had a tone in her voice I'd not heard before. Genuine fear. And I could tell it wasn't about the money.

'Really, it's fine.'

It wasn't though. It wasn't fine. That following morning I took Max on the usual route. Through Millfields. Down to the navigation. On my back was a rucksack full of unopened mail. I decided my only recourse was to bury it somewhere near Angel. I looked up to her. She'd been around longer than I had. She provided the city with energy, with life, for god's sake. Surely she'd know what to do about a trivial matter like this.

As I reached the entrance, I was surprised to see one of my narrowboat friends up and about, a rollie glued to her bottom lip. It wasn't even nine a.m. She clutched what looked like a plastic cup of wine.

I was even more surprised when she spoke to me.

'You're the pylon guy, right?'

'Pardon?'

'The pylon guy.'

'I'm not sure I…'

'It's okay,' she said. 'You'd better know. Aaron's back. Says he wants to talk to you.' She gestured towards the filter beds.

'Aaron.'

'Old bloke, hangs around the marsh. You must have seen him. He doesn't stop talking about you, anyway.'

'I don't think I…' I shrugged.

'Her fella,' she said.

Snap. Crack.

Max with a twig in his mouth, grinning.

Me with my heart broken.

7. RIVAL

I entered the filter beds, trembling. She was there, of course. Looking resplendent against a white sky and – I have to say – relieved to see me.

Beneath her a stooped figure waited with a black Labrador. He must have been sixty or more. Grey hair bristled from beneath a baseball cap. His white T-shirt was far too big for him. Even though he was wearing sandals, he had chosen to wear socks, and not even a matching pair. It was hard to make out his facial features, what with my eyes being the way they were. But I could see what looked like egg stains in his beard, and down his chest. Or maybe it was phlegm. He had a dirty hacking cough.

Look at the state of him, I thought. This Aaron bloke. What the hell is she doing with him?

The dogs circled each other, the Labrador growling.

'He's alright,' said Aaron in a mildly cockney accent. 'He's old. Bit blind in one eye. Gets snappy.'

'Max's sight's not good either.'

'Cataracts,' he said.

'How did you know?'

'Got my own eyes.' I couldn't quite tell, but it felt like he was giving me a conspiratorial wink. I seethed.

After a long pause he said, 'You've come for her, then?'

'I'm sorry?'

'Her.' He jerked his head at Angel. I could sense her flinch. 'Sorry to say, mate, but you don't have long.'

'I'm not sure…'

'You shouldn't be here,' he said. 'It's not your place.'

But the marsh wasn't anyone's place, I reasoned silently. How dare he? I considered hitting him.

'She's not supposed to be here either,' Aaron said. 'I can see why you two get along. Take a look at that.'

He jabbed his stick towards a laminated A4 sign taped beside the pylon. I stared at the text, but my vision was blurred.

'I don't know what it says.'

'They're trying to prettify the marshes. Clean it up. Another excuse for them to get their mitts on things, I reckon. It's all about the money now.'

'But what does the sign actually say?'

'It's a notice of works,' he said. 'They're coming to take her down.'

8. DEATH

There was a time before I fell in love on Hackney Marshes. When things were okay. I wrote ads. I got paid. I was in love with Ruth. We laughed a lot. But I couldn't dwell on the past. I had to think about the here and now.

I tipped the unanswered bank demands from my rucksack and replaced them with tools. Anything I could find.

A hammer. A knife. A spanner.

Ruth knew there was something wrong. With the baby, I mean. And at last the doctors agreed she was right. Sophia had a serious food intolerance problem. Wheat, lactose, gluten, milk, soy, eggs. Whatever Ruth consumed, her breasts would turn into liquid poison.

And there she was thinking everything was my fault.

There was a whole load of medical stuff to read about, apparently, but I couldn't keep my attention on it. Ruth sat me down with the letter from the doctor and told me it was a turning point. Sophia would get better and better from now on.

'Now we can get you the help you need,' she said, rubbing a hand through my hair. My spine tingled. I couldn't remember the last time we touched.

But what help did I need? What the hell could Ruth do about my situation?

They were coming the next morning, contract workers in yellow jackets, with their machinery. And they were going to dismantle Angel, piece by piece. In preparation, they'd erected blue hoardings around the base of her legs. I'd been watching them come and go from a bird hide I'd built in the bushes.

The way they acted around her, laughing, joking. It was disgusting.

If she'd been an old oak, she'd have dozens of hippy tree-huggers chained to her trunk by now. This pylon had stood watch over these beds for decades. She'd kept the city lit, boiled the people's kettles, provided their shitty television programmes, warmed their babies' bottles.

This was the thanks she got.

I was all she had left. That Aaron, he was a flake. Since the day I ran from him in tears, he'd completely vanished. Not a trace. I asked the woman from the narrowboat if she'd seen him.

'Dunno who you're talking about,' she told me, straight-faced.

'The old bloke from the marshes!' I cried. 'Her fella!'

'Sure it was me?'

'Yes, but you were drunk… out of it… maybe you don't remember.'

'Cheeky fuck. You should take a look at yourself, chum.'

Well, what did it matter? Part of me was glad he'd gone. He must have been watching me with her for a long time before he dared to confront us. Once he'd seen how serious we were he'd turned tail and fled. The coward.

Not me. I had a plan.

When darkness came, I put the cataract drops to good use. I could see very clearly as I approached the locked gate of the filter beds and made my ascent. As I dropped, a fox scuttled into the bushes and poked his nose out, thinking I couldn't see him. The fool. I hissed at him. Moved on with my mission.

The hoardings were a trickier climb. It took a few run-ups, but once I had my fingertips over the rim I could pull myself up, using the hinges of the hoarding as a foot grip.

Once on the other side, I settled beside Angel and unpacked my whisky and my tools. I touched her leg. She shivered as if cold. But I knew it wasn't the cold.

'Don't worry,' I reassured her. 'Tk tk tk tk tk tk tsssssssssssssst.'

I wasn't afraid. These jobsworths would hardly risk their safety to tackle an armed man first thing in the morning. They'd have to phone the boss. Call the police. Get the local press down here.

A right big hoo-ha. That's what I expected.

I tried to stay awake but the whisky overpowered me. It was only an engine and the chatter of workmen that alerted me the next morning. I scrabbled to my feet and peered through a slit in the hoarding.

There were four of them climbing out, and beyond, a white van approaching. Almost certainly there would be more of them inside.

A hot sun beat down. My heart was tight. I clenched the spanner. I breathed deeply and slowly.

I waited.

THENAR SPACE

div-uh-ney-shuh-n (noun)
1. the practice of attempting to foretell future events or discover hidden knowledge by occult or supernatural means;
2. augury; prophecy;
3. perception by intuition; instinctive foresight.

Her real name is Lotte but they call her the Trolley Div. She knows it because she hears it said. The teenagers who drift into the supermarket after school for cans of pop. The skateboard kids who come at dusk. Even grownups who should know better. Big men with fat necks from the delivery trucks. Snarky young mums with pushchairs smoking fags. They have all said it, from time to time, within earshot.

'Watch out for the Trolley Div.'

'Trolley Div's comin'.'

'Pssst, check out the Trolley Div. Bloody hell. The face on her.'

Even the ones who don't say it, the polite ones, the casual shoppers, the out-of-towners, they look like they're thinking it. And if not Trolley Div, then whatever it is they call people who collect shopping trolleys in supermarket car parks.

Trolley Spod. Trolley Bod. Trolley Spaz. Trolley Tart. Trolley Troll.

Maybe they don't have a special name for them. Only a sense that trolley attendants are somehow lesser beings. Stupid. Failed. Unqualified. Bottom of the pile. There to use and abuse, with no ears to hear, no heart to feel, no power at their fingertips with which they could exact their bloody revenge. And Lotte could, you know. She could get her own back on them, easily. When they least expect it, she could send a train of trolleys hurtling in the direction of their shiny cars, their weak flesh, their noisy babies, and crush their bones, burst their skins, ruin their precious paintwork.

But that's not what she's here to do. That's not her destiny.

There's more to this trolley game than shoppers think. More to her than they realise. More to this car park than they can see. But for now she's keeping it close to her chest, hands gripped on the handle, the long chain of interlocked trolleys flexing before her, under control, yet only a microsecond away from chaos. All it takes is a slight change in velocity. One trolley too many at the end of the stack. A sudden shift in weight distribution. Then all hell could break loose, like planets spinning out of the solar system or snooker balls crashing into each other. This event might happen. Probably *will* happen, she suspects. But only when the time is right. At this moment, Lotte cannot see that far ahead.

What she does know is that something is coming. Lotte can tell because of a peculiar phenomenon in which she keeps finding trolleys abandoned in the same arrangement at the same time of day, around three p.m. It took her a while to notice, but she's sure it is happening and she isn't imagining it, not that she'd dare tell anyone at work. Most of the staff treat her like she's mentally challenged. This would only make it worse. But she has eyes in her head and she can see what's in front of her: a clear pattern that repeats itself every day.

There's always a trolley out by the recycling area with bins for clothes, bottles and cans. Then there's a sequence of two more trolleys interspersed between car clusters, leading to the zebra crossing by the entrance. There she finds one of those big, deep trolleys with plastic seats for kiddies. From this point, the pattern forks into two lines of four trolleys. Always four in each. At the end of one prong, there's a trolley by the traffic island at the exit with the sign that says, 'See you again!' At the end of the other prong, two trolleys huddled by the hedgerow that separates the car park from the main road. There are always twelve trolleys in the arrangement, all pointing in the same direction, narrow ends angled towards the superstore doors, as if magnetically charged.

Lotte doesn't know what exactly the pattern means but it suggests to her that there will be a time of reckoning, and soon.

This might be a good thing. After all, it was a day of reckoning that led to her getting this job two years ago. One of the friendlier till staff, a girl called Iga, told Lotte that her predecessor wasn't properly trained. They didn't tell him that he was not allowed to push a stack of more than eight trolleys. Ended up pushing ten one day when the stack began to waggle and swerve until he lost control and crunched into a van, shattering his shoulder. That was the end of that. Permanent damage to his tendons. He got lawyers involved and there was a big hoo-ha about it. A nasty fight that was still ongoing.

In the meantime, the supermarket needed someone to collect trolleys from the bays and gather the abandoned ones from the nether regions of the car park. Someone had to keep the stacks by the door replenished for shoppers on their way in. So the marketing people put an advert in the paper and Lotte applied, at the suggestion of her Nana, with encouragement from the social worker who checked on them from time to time, because Nana was harder to care for as she got older and the bad people in the government were cutting everything that helped – snip! snip! snip!

They desperately needed money but Lotte had problems with the whole *getting money* thing. Nothing big. But she'd not worked since she left school at sixteen and wasn't exactly cut out for one of those offices with all those people in suits.

It's not that she's dumb. Lotte knows all the constellations. The names of galaxies. The distances between planets. She can sense the tilt of the Earth. Smell the onset of seasons. Feel instinctively what the weather will be like this week. She knows the names of every plant in the park, of all the muscles in her body and the bones they connect. But she has trouble with reading and maths, and with talking to non-Nana people or understanding what they mean. In turn, non-Nana people find Lotte odd with her stooped back and heavy brow, a touch of something doctors call 'frontal bossing'.

Problems, problems. Nothing major, nothing that need stop you, Nana says, just you have to work harder that is all. You have a bigger mountain to climb. But you have abilities, Nana says, a way of seeing, only people don't know it yet. They haven't caught up with you. In that way, it is they who have special needs.

When Lotte got the trolley attendant job, it was something of a surprise. They celebrated with chocolate cake and a mushroom brew. Then they did some loud chanting and rune casting like the old days before the social services told them to stop it for the sake of Lotte's future.

'You have found your role at last,' Nana said, raising her chipped mug of hallucinogenic tea, 'your magical quest begins here.'

Alan, her manager at the supermarket, has made a bit more effort with training Lotte than he did with her predecessor. He follows the new handbook distributed nationwide to make sure no more trolley attendants get smashed up. But he's a lazy guy. He's been to university and it seems like he doesn't really want to be a supermarket trainee manager. He's in a band. Writing a novel. Car parks and car park attendants are a bit beneath a man of his talents. Alan hasn't checked on Lotte much since her probation period ended, when her pay went up from £8 an hour to £8.50. Not bad for a twenty-one-year-old Trolley Div. If all goes well she might get promoted to *car park porter*, a much more important job, helping shoppers with bags, directing cars to empty lots at busy times and showing folk to specialist trolleys and electric scooters. It means dealing with strangers, which gives her butterflies, but it pays £9 per hour.

It's this promise of more money that first encouraged her to add another trolley to the eight-trolley limit. It wasn't too hard once she got used to the increased swerve and thrust. Nobody really noticed or cared. And with each additional trolley Lotte has become more efficient at her job. Long stacks of nine, ten, even eleven. She can guide them to the store entrance, rain or shine. It's no longer the lure of a promotion or extra income that motivates her to test the limits of the trolleys in this way. It's a feeling. Like an urge, or something she is supposed to do.

A calling.

Besides, there is little else for her to think about at work, other than the propulsion of the trolley train and its relationship to the many hazards: parked cars, pedestrians and incoming traffic. Her job may look easy to those shoppers who push past her with grunts and harrumphs, but there are multiple complex factors of which she must be constantly aware. The swivel of wheels. The undulations of tarmac. The placements of speed bumps and rain gutters. The welts of road markings. Lotte has learned the delicate dance of velocity, direction and momentum. She can sense the shifts of the trolley train in the tug of finger muscles and the pressure on that bit of her hand where the handle fits into the curve between thumb and forefinger, known as the 'thenar space'. At first these muscles ached with strain but gradually they've become attuned. Now the thenar space is her ultimate sensor, a way of reading the world in motion. She could probably do her job blindfolded if it ever comes down to it. If a crazed villain leapt from a car and stabbed out her eyes with a Bic biro, she could still negotiate the twists and turns of the car park, using only her memory and the instincts in her thenar space.

But life is not always so easily predicable. Lotte knows this too well. Things can happen outside your control.

Pushing a wobbly line of trolleys through a busy car park leaves her exposed to 'random' factors, as she calls them, but always in her mind with inverted commas, like when you say something you don't necessarily mean, or that other people say but you don't necessarily believe. As Nana says, nothing is truly random.

A 'random' describes anything not factored into her calculations that might disrupt the flow of motion. A crushed Coke can, discarded, trapped beneath a wheel, might cause the trolley train to skid. That's an example of a 'random'. After all, who could predict the decision of a person to purchase a Coke, the speedy guzzling of the drink and the decision to toss the can away? You'd have to predict the power and angle of the toss to work out the landing place. Then a passing teenager might kick the can, sending it skittering into the path of Lotte's trolleys as she approached. That would entail a load of 'randoms' happening faster than the human brain could process.

There are more examples, too. A patch of ice in winter. A stray cardboard box, blown by the wind. A freshly formed crack in the concrete. Perhaps one of those big SUVs, parked badly, could scupper Lotte's calculations of the turning angle so that her trolleys go into the back of a Porsche or right up an old lady's bottom. Worse, a toddler might run out from behind a car and end Lotte's career. The child would die, crushed beneath her wheels, and Lotte would hide behind a tree in the cemetery, watching the funeral, murmuring 'sorry' over and over, before the police led her back to the car and took her to prison for the rest of her life.

Every day Lotte lives with these possibilities. Every moment has violent potential. Each millisecond life can go in a million different directions. And sometimes, just sometimes, a person gets to be the guiding hand. This is something a man in a suit doing wordy, numbery gubbins on a computer will never understand. The weight of responsibility. The understanding that anyone can be an agent of the universe. Even a Trolley Div.

At primary school, long before she became Trolley Div, they called her 'Not-A-Lotte' and 'Toi-Lotte' and 'Fat Botty'. She was the awkward kid, the freak, the slowcoach. It didn't matter how many times Nana complained to teachers or lingered at the gates, taking swipes at her classmates' heads as they left school, Lotte was excluded from their games. Then one day they played 'trains'. A child would run around the playground with another child holding onto their coat tail. Then another child would latch on, then another, then another. On and on this went until there were ten, twelve, maybe fifteen kids in a weaving line. It didn't matter who joined the train, only that it kept getting longer. It was a case of *the more the merrier*. So Lotte seized her chance. She grasped onto the last child's coat and ran, pulled faster by the train as it weaved and twisted, at a speed she could never achieve under her own steam. Wind in her face, she laughed with a momentary joy, moving as part of a greater whole. Then the leading child changed directions sharply and the line whip-cracked. Lotte lost her grip and flew out, tripping headfirst onto the concrete.

Her schoolmates laughed as she got back on her feet, weeping with pain and spitting out tiny white flecks of enamel. Her front teeth were chipped. It was something she never got fixed, for Nana doesn't trust the medical establishment, dentists included. Whenever Lotte's teeth hurt, Nana would give her a gluey mixture of cloves and garlic to chew. These days a few of her teeth are missing. A few more are rotten. But her chipped incisors are still there, bucked, prominent and rough to the tongue. A legacy of that unfortunate event.

Only now Lotte understands that it was no random incident but a valuable lesson that has finally come to fruition. For today she controls her own train. Except this one is not made up of children. This one is made from plastic and steel and she, Lotte Dugmore, has sole influence over its direction, with full responsibility for what might happen because of it, and to whom. Thanks to that childhood experience of whiplash, she knows there are three phases to its motion. First, a sudden reversal in direction, which takes only a small jerk of her hands on the trolley handle. Next, a wave of momentum runs through the chain, bending in the middle, becoming a bigger bend towards the end and – finally – a whiplash strikes with force.

All this power unleashed by a twitch of her thenar space.

A similar twitch might have afflicted her father's hand fifteen years ago on the M6 motorway. If not, then what else could have caused the accident? Why else would he lose control in the blink of an eye? There must have been a sudden involuntary spasm where her father's thumb and forefinger met the steering wheel, which sent the family car veering from its lane into the barrier – BANG! – then spinning, spinning, with all those vehicles crunching after, so much smoke and noise, and she a child in the back seat among the carnage, the only thing alive in their Renault at the end of it all. Six people dead, including her parents. All because of thenar space.

Lotte now has that same power which her dead father once possessed. When the time comes, she will use it for good, or perhaps evil, or something in between. She doesn't know. But whatever it is, it must have a connection to the strange alignment of trolleys she finds in her mid-afternoon collection. Always twelve in a distinct pattern that she draws with a pencil onto a piece of paper to show her Nana that evening. Nana who knows about these things and who never disappoints.

At the sight of Lotte's little diagram, Nana's eyes widen. 'I know that shape,' she says, 'and so do you, Lotte, my dear. For it is the constellation of Perseus.'

Nana gets out a book and shows her:

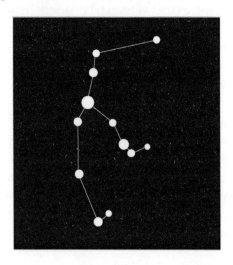

She's right as well. Almost trolley for trolley, the pattern is the same. Lotte notices that the big star near the middle is that bit at the zebra crossing, which leads shoppers to the entrance from the central pedestrian strip with its pretty saplings. That is where she always finds the deep trolley with the kiddie seats. Nana tells her this star is Algol, the Demon Star, a harbinger of bad fortune. She says that the word 'disaster' literally means 'bad star'.

Dis-*aster*.

Well, that seals it. Something is coming, Lotte is sure of it, but still she doesn't know what, or when. That is until she spots two receipts in adjacent trolleys by the hedgerow one morning. Usually when Lotte sees a receipt she has a little nosey at what people have bought. But this time it's not the list of items that catches her eye. It's the price at the bottom. The first receipt is for £234. The second receipt is for £23.40.

Isn't that an odd coincidence?

If nothing is random, and she's sure that it isn't, then there is meaning in these numbers 2, 3 and 4.

Or 2 and 34.

Or 23 and 4.

It puzzles her for a while before it hits her: 23/4. The 23rd of April. That's it! And it's only a week from now. If something is coming, then it is coming on the 23rd of April. It makes sense. And the only place this future event could happen is Algol, the Demon Star at the centre of the Perseus constellation, located on the zebra crossing at the supermarket entrance. Lotte draws a red cross over Algol on her diagram, circles it, then draws the date *23rd April* in big letters. That night she sleeps with the piece of paper beneath her pillow.

Despite her fear of talking to people at work, Lotte is too excited to keep her secret, so she confides in Iga, the nice checkout girl who finds time to speak to her among the hustle and bustle of backroom tea breaks, where Lotte never feels welcome. Lotte doesn't mention the trolley pattern, which Iga might find too weird. Only that she thinks that at three p.m. on the 23rd they should look out for trouble near the entrance, because the stars are never wrong.

Iga smiles and nods. 'You must keep watch, Lotte, it's important. Don't let people down.'

And Lotte won't, she swears she won't. She swears this under her breath every night as she lies in bed in their living room with the diagram safe beneath her head, Nana snoring beyond the flimsy partition. They've always slept this way because the flat has only one bedroom, which is where Nana keeps her books on witchcraft, tarot and astrology, stacked so high and deep you can barely get through the door. It used to annoy Lotte, at times, when she was a teenager. Seemed unfair.

Not any more.

Thanks to this deep knowledge which Nana has gathered over the years, Lotte can finally do something special in her life and become a respected car park porter, worth £9 per hour. If that's her reward for sleeping beneath a sideboard, so be it. Not that she hasn't enhanced her cramped space with personal touches. A large, colourful chart of the human body, showing the tissues, veins and bones. A mobile hung from the ceiling with the planets of the solar system spinning around a yellow sun. A doll's house in which Lotte likes to arrange effigies of her parents. Sometimes they're sat at the kitchen table. Sometimes lain in bed. Sometimes they're screaming in terror from the top window because of a chip pan fire that's filled the house with smoke (Lotte uses Nana's incense sticks for effect). Other times they stand at the front door, waving proudly as Lotte heads off to work.

Her mother and father have never been so proud as on the 23rd of April when Lotte leaves the flat, nerves jangling. Throughout the morning she's too excited to concentrate on the job, which is tough because it's a busy day. Lots of customers leaving their trolleys willy-nilly instead of in the bays where they are supposed to. There's hustle and bustle by the entrance because a bald man is handing out leaflets about the AA and Cub Scouts are collecting for charity. The customers try to avoid them by cramming through the left-hand sliding door instead of using both exits, causing a right nuisance as Lotte tries to keep the trolleys stacked up neatly.

Honestly!

After lunch, Alan the manager sends Lotte out back to the delivery area to help clean up a spill after a forklift driver drops a pallet of milk. It takes ages and the men make her go and get them tea from the machine while they smoke and tell rude jokes. This jeopardises the timings. Tick, tock, tick, tock. It's nearly three p.m. by the time she hurries around the side of the store, past the staff smoking area and into the car park. Almost instantly, she hears a cry of 'Help!'

It's happening, it's happening.

Heart in her mouth, Lotte runs towards the zebra crossing. But there's something amiss. She feels utterly useless without a trolley train at her command. What can she actually *do*? She has nothing with which to unleash hell on whatever she's about to encounter. This is not how she envisioned it. Closer to the store entrance, she's even more uncertain. There's only a woman with a handbag approaching from the avenue of saplings while an old man hobbles through the automatic doors. The crossing is empty, except for something small and brown on the ground. She picks it up. It's a teddy bear with a bandage on its head. A cocktail stick protrudes from its chest, dripping with tomato ketchup.

Lotte hears giggles. She turns to see Iga and a few of the checkout staff stood by the doors, pointing at her.

'You have saved the day,' says Iga. 'The bear will live!'

It's a mean, nasty laugh, not a friendly one. Lotte realises that Iga put the bear there as a joke. It's not nice at all. But worse still, it means that the trolleys were wrong, the stars were wrong, and Nana was wrong. Everything was wrong.

Wrong. Wrong. Wrong.

What was she thinking?

She is, after all, just a Trolley Div.

A stupid, stupid Trolley Div.

* * *

Lotte doesn't eat for a week. Not much, anyway. A bit of Nana's stew. Some turnip soup. A spoon of raw honey here and there. At work she talks to nobody, and certainly not Iga. Sometimes Alan asks her if she is okay but he only does this because he's the manager and wants to look good for the human resources people.

He doesn't care.

Nobody cares except for Nana, who says, 'Don't let them get you down. You must trust your second sight, Lotte, not everyone has it. Like anything important in life, you won't get it right from the get-go. Maybe you see pieces of a puzzle but not how they fit together.'

Lotte lies awake at night beneath the dangling cardboard planets as Nana snores, imagining what her parents would say to make her feel better, had her dad not driven them to their deaths.

Did he really lose control, just like that?

She wonders how come she, Lotte Dugmore, can manoeuvre up to twenty trolleys around a car park full of people and traffic and kids and pigeons and Coke cans and never crash once. Not even once!

Lotte leans from her bed and peers into the bedroom of the doll's house, where her mum sits alone on the bed.

'Oh, Lotte, we both loved you so much and we worked hard to get you things you needed. Pretty things to wear. Delicious things to eat. A roof to keep the rain away. Warm radiators in winter. They all cost money, such a lot of money. Your dad worked nights and sometimes when he came home he drank beer to switch off, to settle down, to get some sleep. Each morning he'd drink for a bit longer, and longer, and longer, until it became a habit. A bad habit, I know. But the stress, Lotte, the stress. Don't blame him. It's hard being a grownup. All we wanted was the best for you. Then we got a call one morning to say that your Nana had fallen over. She was in hospital. She really needed us. So your dad and I put you in the back seat and we all drove up the motorway, full of worry, even though your dad had not slept, even though he'd drunk a few beers after work, as usual. Maybe it was more than a few, but it was a habit, so he didn't think much about it. He lost control out of love. Out of love for Nana. Out of love for you. Daddy made a mistake at the wheel and we lost control. But you can get it back, Lotte, I know it. You have found your calling at last. The car park is a place where you can shine like a star. We even named you Lotte, as in *car lot*. Don't you see? Can you understand now? It's your destiny!'

Her mother's words inspire Lotte. They lift her spirits. She returns to work full of hope, back to her old self again, with her eyes wide open and that train of trolleys stretching out before her, like a flash forward to the near future.

Almost immediately, the car park offers up its mysteries once more. On an otherwise uneventful day in early June, Lotte is delighted to find the trolleys laid out in the very same stellar pattern as before. There's one left by the recycling bins, then that familiar sequence of trolleys which splits by the zebra crossing into two prongs, just like the constellation of Perseus. Twelve trolleys, yet again.

This cannot be the work of sneaky Iga, for Lotte never told her about the trolley pattern. Besides, Iga might be smart and popular but there's no way she knows about constellations, and definitely not Perseus.

Lotte tries to keep her emotions in check this time, but it's hard to contain herself when, only a day after the astronomical manifestation returns, she finds a receipt in a basket left near the cash machines. It's for £2.34. Again, the numbers 2, 3 and 4. This cannot be a coincidence. It simply cannot be chance. But if it's not the 23rd of April she should look out for, then when?

Like Nana says, it's a puzzle. The pieces are there but she can't get them to fit.

Lotte is still wondering about this on Nana's favourite day of the year, the summer solstice, on the 21st of June. In the

1960s Nana used to go to a place called Stonehenge where our ancestors prayed to the Sun on the longest day of the year. Nana would dance around the stones with her friends, eating magic mushrooms and chanting, like she still does these days, except in the flat, because she can't walk any more, and no dancing either, just the mushrooms and chanting. Instead of giant stones there are only Nana's beloved crystals, laid out on the coffee table. As they eat breakfast, even though she's heard it before, Lotte asks Nana to tell her about the solstice, like when she was little, using pictures torn from old books.

Nana duly gets out a crumpled diagram of the solar system, the Earth and the Sun.

'The Earth goes around the Sun to make a year, and tilts to make the seasons,' Nana intones, 'which is what makes things die and grow and change throughout the years. Think about that Lotte, our lives dependent on a little tilt of the Earth, this way and that, bringing heat and cold, light and dark, life and death.'

As Nana speaks, Lotte gasps at the sight of some numbers on the picture. Why didn't she think of this before? The angle of the Earth's tilt today is 23.4 degrees. That's always the angle of the Earth on the day of the summer solstice, which is today, the 21st of June.

All at once, the pieces of the puzzle spin into place.

Lotte's age is twenty-one. The number 21 is 12 backwards. Twelve trolleys. Twelve stars in the constellation of Perseus. Receipts with the numbers 2, 3 and 4. The tilt of the Earth on the 21st of June is 23.4 degrees.

Bingo.

Lotte leaps to her feet, kisses Nana, and is out the door and on the way to work within minutes, gnawing her fingernails with excitement. The receipts for £234, £23.40 and £2.34 never signified the 23rd of April. It was the 21st of June all along. She can see it now, as clear as she can see the roof of the superstore gleam in the sun and the lampposts, tall as trees, above the first parked cars of the day. All she needs to do is stay vigilant, keep the trolley train well-stacked, and let her thenar space guide its locomotion.

The hours pass. Ten o'clock, eleven o'clock, twelve o'clock.

Lotte eats her egg sandwich on the park bench outside the entrance of the superstore, watching traffic crawl through the high street, while pigeons peck at her feet in the brilliant sunshine of the longest day of the year.

Back to the car park and there's a lot of trolleys to collect in the early afternoon. Remnants of the lunchtime rush. People who squeeze in a quick shop during working hours. Or those who try to get it done before they pick up their kids from school. These types are too busy to put their trolleys in the bays but Lotte doesn't mind. She's glad of it. Gives her plenty of trolleys to keep her barrel loaded. She keeps going around and around the car park, never straying too far from the entrance.

At three p.m. she's alert and fully primed. Then three p.m. passes. It becomes 3.05, 3.10, 3.11. Tick, tock, tick, tock. She begins to feel twinges of despair when she notices two cars moving slowly, one after the other, towards the zebra crossing. Much too slowly for her liking. It's as if the first car is deliberately impeding the one behind. Meanwhile, a young lady with a trolley, grinning toddler in the seat, kicking his little legs, exits through the automatic doors.

Lotte can see what's about to happen, as clearly as if it has already happened. She turns her train of eighteen trolleys in an elegant arc, expertly avoiding the bollards by the taxi rank, and moves at pace towards the crossing where the first car has stopped, engine rumbling with menace. She's close enough to read the number plate: CP18 DIV.

Car park. Eighteen trolleys. A Trolley Div.

This is it.

This is it.

Lotte accelerates as the leading car door opens and a burly man with cropped black hair and a white T-shirt gets out. He turns to the car behind, pulling something from the back seat that looks like a weapon – a rifle, shotgun, something like that, she doesn't know much about weapons. Then a man from the car behind gets out and he too reaches for something, probably a gun. This happens in the very moment that the young lady with the toddler steps onto the crossing. She's going to get in the way of whatever is about to happen. They're going to get hurt unless Lotte does something.

Now.

Lotte doesn't need to think. Two years of muscle memory take over as she jerks the handle of the trolley in precisely the right way to whiplash the stack and send the end trolley whizzing along the road, ripples of energy wobbling the air as it tears a rift in space–time. It glances off the young lady's shopping trolley, forcing her to pull back from the crossing with a yelp, safely out of harm's way, then it ricochets into the gunman's backside, spinning him round to face Lotte.

Next, she gives the whole trolley train a hard shove and lets momentum do the rest. The stack rattles sideways like a snake, hitting the man full on, sweeping him from the road. He slams into a brick pillar and crumples beneath a tangle of steel.

The young lady with the toddler screams, 'Bloody maniac!' and Lotte assumes that she is addressing the gunman, even though she's looking right at Lotte. As Lotte gets closer, she sees the man from the second car, stood by the open door, mouth wide open in surprise, holding his wallet.

People rush from the store to see what's going on. Some stop between cars with their shopping bags, heads above the roofs, watching like meercats as Lotte approaches her stricken victim, groaning with pain beneath the trolley stack. It's curious. She cannot see his weapon. No weapon at all. Only a clutch of reusable shopping bags in one of his hands.

He must have dropped the shotgun somewhere. Thrown it away somehow. Blood trickles down his face. His eyes are wild with loathing.

'What the hell!' he yells at her. 'You stupid mong! You crazy fucking bitch!'

The man keeps going on like that, ranting and raving. All kinds of nasty stuff coming out of his mouth as the crowd of onlookers thickens around them. Lotte beams down at him in triumph. Let him yell. Sticks and stones may break her bones but words won't hurt her any more. She's been called worse.

It's of no matter anyway. She has taken control and saved the day. Mum and Dad would burst with pride if they could see her now. She cannot wait to tell Nana when she gets home. And when Alan the manager finds out about this, he's going to be absolutely delighted.

TYRANNOSAURS BASK IN THE WARMTH OF THE ASTEROID

The monkey knows that something is wrong. She's a metre away, behind reinforced glass, leathery lips curled back, baring her buckled teeth. At first, I think she's laughing, but this is not laughter. This is fear.

She's braced for an attack.

I press my nose against the glass. Perhaps it's me she fears, a forty-seven-year-old man. If so, it's a justified terror. We've done our damage to the world, we white men, but I doubt she has singled me out as a particularly egregious threat. The glass is smudged with marks left by the noses, lips and fingertips of many other zoo visitors who have stood in this spot to look at the crested black macaques perched on rootless trees and blocks of artificial rock.

No, it's not me. There's something else. An existential threat that she can sense but which I cannot see. She stares past my shoulder, trembling. Hands tightly grip the rock on which she sits. A torrent of golden piss gushes from her vulva, splashing over her fingers. The other monkeys start to leap up and down, shrieking frantically.

This doesn't seem normal. When I arrived with my daughter this morning, I expected most of the animals to be asleep, or in hiding, which is how I remember zoos from my youth; not freaking out like this. I cannot tell if it's a manifestation of my anxiety or a real phenomenon but there's a tension in the place. When we tried to visit the lemurs, they were racing around their enclosure in a frenzy and we were quickly ushered out. The keepers cancelled the public feeding session, telling the line of parents and toddlers that the lemurs were feeling funny today and needed to let off steam before they settled down for a rest.

Maybe it's the heat. This endless summer drought, longer even than the one we had last year, and the one before that. There's not a cloud in the sky. The sun is bastard hot. I can't stand it myself and I'm not covered in black fur, nor confined behind glass, hands covered in my own piss. Perhaps that's what's wrong with the monkey. But what do I know?

I look at my daughter. She's staring at the monkey too, but with a bored expression, impatient for the next enclosure and the next incarcerated animal.

'It's a crested black macaque,' I say, pointing to the information plaque. 'Endangered.'

Almost all the plaques say *endangered*. This place isn't even a zoo, according to the promotional literature on the website. It's a wildlife refuge for rare animals, born in captivity, unable to return to their felled habitations, their scorched plains and polluted rivers. This crested black macaque is pissing for my entertainment in a glass box in the East Sussex countryside when she should be foraging the jungles of Indonesia; jungles we have hacked down so we can have takeaway coffee cups. To make matters worse, macaque meat is prized by some indigenous peoples, who like to flame roast them whole, then eat the peppery flesh. I've seen pictures on the internet of charred monkeys with rictus grins, like simian Egyptian mummies, piled high on market stall tables beside charred bats and pythons.

I don't tell Molly any of this additional information. She's almost ten, smart as a whip, but still too small, too innocent, to hear the whole truth. I brought her into this world, and I must shield her as best I can. Give her a childhood in which she can be free to wonder and dream, to hope, unburdened by guilt and the crush of information, the awful weight of knowledge. A childhood close to the one I enjoyed, when everyday actions like driving a car, drinking from a plastic bottle and eating a burger did not feel like you were hastening the apocalypse. When visiting a zoo did not feel like you were gawping at the last survivors of a catastrophe for which you were responsible. A time before the sixth great extinction, before the ice caps melted, before antibiotics began to fail and a blood infection took the life of the mother of my only child, leaving me to deal with it all alone these past five years.

I must stop thinking like this, so I have been told, repeatedly, by my friends, my family and my therapist. I must quieten that anxious voice and focus on Molly's happiness. As my wife is no longer around, and I am too unbearable to live with, according to the women I've dated, then it's up to me, and I must become better than the father I am. I try, though, I really try. But it's hard. Other people seem to become fathers effortlessly. They build things with their kids. Take them skateboarding. Bake cakes. Picnic in the park. They look happy, too, like they were born to do it. But I feel like I'm putting on an ill-fitting costume, pretending to be a dad, here at the animal park on the sort of day out I see other people posting on Facebook.

It doesn't help that Molly's an unsociable kid who prefers to sit in her room and read or play computer games. She has a habit of dismissing my suggestions for weekend activities. It saps my motivation a little, trying to sell something to her that not even I want to do, which is why we usually end up kicking around the house, watching *Doctor Who* and eating takeaways. That said, Molly was encouragingly excited this morning as we drove across East Sussex, through the Pevensey Levels, fields baking hard in the heat. The countryside looks good in the sunshine, I admit, even when that sunshine is killing it. The road took us past the Long Man of Wilmington, a chalk outline of a figure etched into the downs, holding a staff in each of his hands.

'A giant with no face,' said Molly. 'And no pants on either, so he's naked, Dad, outside in the nude.'

'It's a hot day,' I said.

I read an alternative theory somewhere that those vertical lines were not staffs but the outline of a door between the physical world and the spirit world. It has stuck with me, that idea, but I never interpret it as a figure entering our realm, nor a guard at the threshold. Instead, all I can see is a figure making a swift exit, arms reaching out to pull the door closed behind him, sealing the portal, leaving it all to hell.

Don't go there, he tells the other spirits. *Go anywhere but that fucking place.*

Shortly after the Long Man vanished into the folds of the hills, the zoo appeared, set a little way off the road, among the parched fields. My daughter laughed at the plastic giraffe peering over the hedgerow, a sign for Wellesbury Animal Park hung around its neck. The car park was already busy, so we parked in the gravel overspill area, then joined a queue of people in T-shirts, shorts, flip-flops and summer dresses, carrying rolled-up towels and picnic bags, Instagramming each other with thumbs up, pouting.

I gritted my teeth and held Molly's hand tight, trying to focus for once on the here and now, so I could treasure a moment with my daughter and inhabit it properly, see the magic of the world through a child's eyes, where the past is just a story, and the future is so far away that it might as well not exist.

* * *

Molly has had enough of the macaques and their nervy antics. She leads me down the corridor and out to the open-air pens, past the beaver enclosure and the flamingos, wings clipped, amassed by a concrete pond. Next door, a giant anteater does laps of a scrubby lawn, its long snout curving into the dusty corners of the perimeter wall.

Molly squeals with delight. 'Look at its funny head!'

I am surprised by the sheer heft of a beast that feasts on tiny insects. Its oversized forelegs and claws are so destructive that it must curl them up and walk on its knuckles. The anteater is moving at a quick pace. Not foraging for food but obsessively lapping its habitat. Occasionally it staggers slightly, as if drunk in the heat. There is some shade beneath a tree, but the anteater keeps on moving.

Over the back fence of the enclosure is the car park and the A27, hissing with weekend traffic and hazy with pollution. The anteater is no more aware of what is beyond the fence than I am of thriving alien planets or alternative multiverses. A supreme entity might be observing us humans right now in the same way I observe this anteater, unaware of our incarceration and the limits of our perception. We live in a planetary prison that we chose to pave over with concrete, choking on fumes.

There I go again. *Compulsive melancholy*, my late wife called it. A form of OCD, says my therapist, an obsessive repetition of negative thoughts that my psyche uses as a weapon against itself, like an autoimmune disease of the imagination. But I'm not so sure about that. At times I feel as if I see things closer to how they really are; rather than me wilfully looking on the dark side of life, it might be that most people are wilfully blinding themselves to the truth. After all, I'm not making things up. The ice caps really are melting. The weather really is weird. Britain really is in another crippling recession. Our civilisation really is in an inexorable decline. I really am losing clients for my graphic design business. My wife really did die of an antibiotic-resistant infection. The newspapers might have used words like 'freak' and 'virulent strain' but there have been others since. Other fathers, other mothers, other sons, other daughters.

This is not a groundless anxiety from which I suffer. I don't see problems that don't exist. These are objective truths; there are statistics and measurements to back it up. It's all actually happening. If others aren't experiencing stressful reactions to the situation, then it's a flaw in their psychological makeup, not mine.

'Dad, do you think Mr Anteater has a funny head?' says Molly.

'It's absolutely hilarious,' I reply.

Between the zoo and the theme park section of Wellesbury Animal Park, there's a miniature bandstand with a gang of animatronic animals on it: mandrill, lemur, python, vulture, alligator, tarantula. Molly hits a button and the animals jiggle from side to side, jaws flapping open, singing in vibrato voices, 'Carnivores swing, herbivores jive, the food chain keeps us alive!'

The robot animals have seen better days. Threadbare fur and rickety mechanics. There's something awry with the mandrill's jaw. It keeps falling open too far, then getting stuck, vibrating and clicking as if it's about to snap off. The audio track crackles hoarsely through clapped-out speakers as the animals sing: 'We are happy happy jungle friends, let us hope life never ends.' Even Molly looks disturbed.

'Let's go and eat lunch,' I say.

In front of the cafe, the picnic benches are heaving with people, their skin red with sunburn. Some loll about on a verge of yellow grass almost turned to hay. Others line up for attractions: an inflatable slide, tin can alley, teacup ride. With a piercing whistle, Thomas the Tank Engine chugs to a stop at the miniature railway platform and families pile off the carriages as the tinkly piano theme song blasts from a tannoy. I shudder at the sight of Thomas's tortured face on the front of the train, human flesh stretched and grafted onto steel, a mutant cyborg enslaved by fat controllers. Molly was banned from watching it as a toddler, not that she wanted to, thank god, innately understanding the implications of its diabolical body horror.

We find a space among sprawled families on a lawn between the entrance to the Adventure Maze and the Costa kiosk, where we sit with our pre-packed sandwiches. As Molly regales me with an overly complicated argument about why we should buy a pug, I notice a black cloud behind the theme park, incongruous against the brilliant blue expanse. No, not a cloud but smoke. Smoke, fed by a line of black curling upward, a dark scar, yellowing the sky on either side of it. A farmer perhaps, burning some waste, a barbeque out of control, or merely the fracked earth of Sussex coughing up a lung. I find it mesmerising, the slow, creeping stain.

I lose the thread of Molly's argument completely, not that it matters, as her voice is being drowned out by the amplified flatulence of a life-size fibreglass Indian elephant on the nearby footpath. It makes a trumpeting noise when people press the yellow button and a farting noise when they press the brown button. Every passing child presses the brown button. Molly sniggers each time and wafts her hand near my backside. After a while I cannot take it. I throw our remaining snacks into our backpack.

'We'll go someplace else,' I tell Molly. She shrugs and sighs deeply, like this happens all the time. Which it does, I suppose, come to think of it. But I cannot help it.

Through a corridor of soft-toy shops and arcade games, we pass from the picnic area into the adventure playground zone and sit on a bench outside the GET SOAKED waterpark where artificial geysers spurt, kids shoot each other with plastic jet-guns and a red slide spirals into a paddling pool. The waterpark is packed with revellers in trunks and bikinis. Naked toddlers. Grandparents in white hats eating ice cream. Teenage girls drinking slushies from oversized plastic containers. The air fills with squeals and laughter, punctuated by the odd gruff shout as a child gets admonished. It's the sound of life going on for other people, as if they exist beyond an invisible partition, separate from me. I know this is how Molly feels too, sometimes, and I wonder if it's my fault, or her mother's fault for dying young, or the fault of society's historical abuse of antibiotics, or if that's just what we're like, me and her.

It's early afternoon and the sun is high, with a warm breeze offering little respite. The few remnants of shade are cast in hard angles against the concrete and plastic. Many people huddle beneath the slide to stop burning in the sunshine. I try to understand how the park can operate these fountains when there's a hosepipe ban on. I assume it's the same water going around and around, gathering more traces of suntan lotion, sweat and child piss with every cycle.

I cannot eat any more of this sandwich. I feel sick.

Molly seems bored, eating her crisps, gazing longingly at the gangways, ropes and slides of the adventure playground, full of children running in madcap circles and screaming with faux fear.

'You can go and play if you like,' I tell her. 'Meet me back at this bench. If I'm not here, wait for me.' She nods. Smiles wanly. Then skips off to the wooden fort structure in the centre of the network and disappears inside its ramparts. Moments later, she's on the wobbly rope bridge between two towers, waving down at me. There are some other kids loitering on the bridge, but I doubt she'll make friends with them. She rarely does. It makes me sad. She's a victim of both genetics and circumstance.

The smoke is now overhead, black clumps of spiralling charcoal, emitting wisps, trailing from a column that's thickening and darkening. The sky is turning rapidly from blue to orange, casting a sepia hue over the zoo, like an Instagram filter. Nobody seems to care, and I assume it must be from a distant bonfire, perhaps a house on fire in a nearby village. But it seems a lot closer than that, only a few fields away, though I find it hard to measure distances at the best of times. It's quite worrying to look at, but worrying is what I resolutely wanted to avoid today, for my daughter's sake.

'Molly!' I yell up into the interior of the adventure playground's central fort. 'I'll be back in a minute!'

'Okay, Dad.' A distant cry from above, but she sounds happy enough.

I return through the corridor of shops, looking for the toilet. On the way, I notice there's a security guard in the soft toy emporium, talking to the woman behind the counter. I slip inside the shop, pretending to look at some fluffy lemurs, and eavesdrop on the conversation, assuming they're discussing the smoke. But they're talking about one of their fellow staff members, who has allegedly been talking behind people's backs, something they're keen to discuss behind her back.

'Excuse me,' I say. 'What's going on with that smoke?'

The security guard shrugs. 'Fire in a field.'

'Is it close?'

'Oh, it's a way away.'

A way away?

One of the quirks of my anxiety is that I constantly look to people for reassurance and yet never believe their comforting words. However, when I come across people who are utterly oblivious to any sense of a problem at all, like these two staff members, I find it disarming, making me feel silly for harbouring a concern, like my woes are entirely fictional.

They return to their conversation and I continue to the toilets near the Thomas the Tank Engine railway. When I emerge, the sky looks radically different. Gone are the black wisps. The smoke has unfolded like two great moth wings, with a dense brown thorax core that intensifies with every passing second. Next to it is what looks to be another source of smoke, a separate feeder channel pumping more noxious gasses into the swirling whole. I glance around, seeking signs of concern, but people are eating ice creams, queuing for chips and sauntering between attractions. A staff member with a walkie-talkie is nattering happily with the litter-picking guy.

Clearly there's nothing wrong.

But, clearly, there is something very wrong.

Where is the smoke coming from?

Molly will be alright for a few more minutes so I hurry across the picnic area, past the farting elephant, to the perimeter hedgerow. As I approach, the air becomes palpably hotter. Above me, the clouds of smoke seethe into each other, giving birth to a denser mass that is beginning to block out the sun, rolling like thundercloud across the zoo enclosures, out towards the levels. Nearby there's a skinny young security guard in a white shirt, shifting uneasily, turning his gaze between me and the smoke.

'What's happening?' I ask.

'Oh, it's a fire in the field,' he says, overly casually. 'We're keeping an eye on it. Should be fine.' He doesn't seem certain. Bites his lip. I am sure that I can hear the crackling of flames.

'John, mate! John!' another security guard jogs into view, clutching his walkie-talkie. When he sees me, he stops dead in his tracks. Beckons his colleague over. Whispers something in his ear. They turn and run to the office building near the turnstiles. A fire engine siren whines in the far distance.

Repressing my panic with deep, measured breaths, I return to the main complex, walking at pace towards the cafe area and adventure playground, back to Molly. Suddenly she seems very far away, as if the ground is stretching beneath me, the earth pulling us further apart. The heat on my back intensifies even though I am increasing my distance from the source. I weave through folk still queuing and eating and bickering with their kids beneath a vast orange mass that is rapidly absorbing all the blue from the sky.

I pass by a covered area where people can stand and vape, not unlike one of the zoo's animal enclosures. Inside, three men stand docile in a haze of vanilla steam. They can definitely see the smoke canopy billowing over us, because one of them points up at it, and the others follow the line of his finger, nodding. They laugh. Clearly they don't think it's worth worrying about, but I'm losing trust in the nonchalance of others and I'm determined to leave as soon as possible.

Shouting my daughter's name over and over, I push through the arcade game players and out into the adventure area, where giggling kids run around the base of the wooden fort.

'Molly!' I shout up into the structure. I can see a few bare legs dangling but cannot tell if it's her or not. 'Please Molly, I need you down here now.'

No answer. I climb the ladder onto the first platform. Then squeeze up through a hatch to the second, where the rigging takes me up past a couple of bewildered boys playing with action figures. They look startled momentarily then go back to their game. Eventually, I'm at the top turret, poking my head out like a tank commander. There's no sign of Molly, but I can now see clearly across the animal park, where there is a wall of fire in the adjacent field, a red tidal wave at breaking point, moments away from crashing onto the perimeter hedge.

This is what it must like after the ship hits the iceberg. That strangely serene period when it is afloat, as it should be, and yet fatally compromised, doomed to sink.

I cry out Molly's name again when I see three kids below, one of whom is her, I'm certain, heading towards the monkey enclosures. I clatter down the rigging, scuffing my knees and shins, jumping from the bottom platform onto wood-chippings. As I jog past the water park, I see that people are beginning to look up at the sky. A rising hubbub of nervous voices. Outbreaks of frantic activity. Parents gather up clothes, rub their children dry, jab at their phones looking for information.

Entering the monkey enclosures, I see Molly stood with a couple of older girls by the mini-bandstand of animatronic animals, whacking the buttons and howling with laughter at the mandrill with the broken jaw, which is now dangling from a piece of wire.

I grab her hand but she pulls away, disgusted. 'Dad!'

'We need to go now, Molly!' I tell her.

She curdles with embarrassment. 'No.'

'Look up, Molly, look up.'

As she looks, her expression softens, as if she finally sees the smoke, or rather, comprehends what the smoke means. She takes my hand.

'Find your parents,' I tell her companions, then I lead Molly in a brisk walk through enclosures of antagonised animals, circling, leaping, screeching. We pass red pandas, meerkats, capuchin monkeys, rock hyraxes and capybaras, all trapped behind glass, aware yet powerless, and out onto the main pathway, where a model of a Tyrannosaurus rex guards the turnstiles.

The breeze has strengthened into a wind, carrying the smoke far across the Sussex sky. There is no longer any sunshine, only the hint of a pale disc casting an ochre glare on the gravel as we hurry through the car park. There are others out here too, clambering into their cars, reversing out. I curse our luck at being parked so far away in the overspill area. I pull harder at Molly's arm, breaking into a jog, as shouts and calls rise from the zoo behind and sirens cry out in the distance.

By the time we reach our car, feathery grey snowflakes of ash have begun to fall. Molly brushes them from her hair and gets into the back seat. A shambling mass of people pours from the zoo, dragging kids and pushchairs. A queue of cars already snakes around the access road. We're going to have to move quickly if we want to leave.

Our tyres crunch on stones as I manoeuvre through a gap in the lines of parked cars, but it makes no difference. We soon come to a stop, and as more vehicles mobilise from their positions closer to the exit, we gain only a yard or two every five minutes. I flick on the wipers to keep the windscreen clear of ash but it falls thicker and thicker.

The slow pace is a torment. Fortunately, Molly doesn't yet realise the extent of the danger. She sits, bewildered, staring out, asking me when we'll get to the road, complaining that she's hungry. I turn on some classical music and talk softly about what we're going to have to eat later. Maybe pizza from the takeaway, any toppings she likes. Even ice cream. A tub each. I struggle to keep the fear from my voice as I see flames startlingly close to the zoo buildings and the steel structures of the ape houses and aviaries, the fire whipped along by rising wind and brittle vegetation.

'Are the animals going to be alright, Dad?' Molly asks, face pressed against the window.

'I don't know.' I fight back tears. 'The zoo has procedures.' It's all I can think of to say. Staff members are amassed by the emergency assembly point near the entrance, but this has taken them by surprise and the situation is escalating rapidly. They don't know what to do about the burgeoning mass of cars trying to leave through the same narrow exit onto a single lane road.

A woman in a hi-vis jacket tries to help fleeing pedestrians pass through the grumbling mass of vehicles but she's getting abuse from panicking drivers. Horns blast but nobody has any power to move faster. In order for us to leave, we must approach the zoo entrance before we can turn right, taking us closer to the inferno. It's as if we are at a diabolical drive-in. The low brown buildings in front of us are crested with a backdrop of belching flame. To the left, the top of a netted enclosure is visible above the fence. I see something flit upwards like a firework, a bird maybe, or a small monkey, before it falls away.

A cacophony erupts. The bleats and howls of terrified animals in the heat of the blaze. Smoke plumes burst from shattering windows. There's a whoosh and crack as one of the fences beside the main building crashes down. Molly screams as the giant anteater staggers through the gap, flames roaring from its back, hind legs dragging. It gets only a few yards before it buckles and hits the gravel in a smouldering heap. Molly screams again.

'Fuck this.' I pull the car to the side of the road, switch off the engine, and kick open the door. I lift Molly from the back seat. She's grown a lot bigger this past year, but I can still carry her. I can still hold her and tell her I love her and that I will look after her, like I did the morning her mother died. I can stop her from watching this horror, at least for today.

'It's okay, sweetheart, we're going home now.'

I turn away from the zoo and march with my daughter in my arms, through lines of cars in the snowing ash, towards the wide green fields beyond the A27, where I know we shall find a fragile sanctuary.

THE LEVELS

1. THE DEAD CYCLIST

The girl from the farm found the dead cyclist on a single lane road to Rickney on the Pevensey Levels. He lay awkwardly, arms buckled beneath his torso, head twisted, eyes in a frozen stare across the tarmac. The girl was certain that he was a cyclist because he wore a luminescent yellow vest and Lycra shorts, but she could see no bike.

She first called 999, and then her dad, who kept vigil with her until the police arrived. A tall, fierce woman introduced herself as Inspector Ramsden. She paced around the dead cyclist, tutting loudly, as her officers scoured the hedgerows for the missing bicycle. It was a curious scene. Ramsden presumed this dead cyclist on the roadside was the result of a hit-and-run, but he was soaking wet, his fingers wrinkled, face bloated. As she crouched beside him, a bead of water seeped from the corner of his mouth. It was a hot July day and there had been no rain for over two weeks. A drought, they said on the news. But they said that every year, as if a drought was a freak event and not just what the normal weather was now.

What was she missing here?

Ramsden removed her shoes and clambered onto the bonnet of the police car to get a look at the bigger picture.

'Ma'am,' protested the driver.

'Pipe down.' Ramsden gazed north across fields striated with drainage ditches, towards an escarpment where the domes of the old Royal Greenwich Observatory pushed above the trees. She swivelled slowly, taking in the vast green lowland, scattered with sheep, telegraph poles and farmhouses, out towards Pevensey Castle and the sea.

She knew this place well. As a teenager, she and her best mate would sometimes cycle out here on a Saturday in summer to while away the hours with a packet of ten Marlboros and a bottle of Coke laced with vodka. They would tramp across the fields, jeering at sheep, then spy on farm boys for a while, choosing which one they'd do. But when winter came, the Levels became too soggy and waterlogged to bother with. Floods were common. This happened more often in recent years, as rising seas and storm tides battered the East Sussex coastline, threatening to revert the lowland to the tidal bay it had been in Roman times. But this month the Levels were as dry as she'd ever known them. There was no watery ditch nearby into which the cyclist could have pitched. They weren't even in a particularly low-lying area. The field behind the body was one of several elevations dotted across the Levels, formerly islands in a lagoon at high tide. Anglo-Saxons built dwellings on them when they began to reclaim the marsh for crops and salt panning. Later, they became medieval villages. You could tell which ones they were from the *–eye* or *–ey* at the end of the name: Chilley, Southeye, Northeye. Where she now stood was at the foot of the abandoned village of Horse Eye, a stepped green hillock in the flatland, demarked by ridges and undulations where there had been houses and tracks.

Ramsden slid from the bonnet and put on her shoes. The girl from the farm was with Constable Hasan, explaining that she was driving her mum's car to Hailsham when she spotted the body. A dark stain on the road surface, which she assumed to be spilled blood, turned out to be water. This had quickly evaporated in the sunshine, indicating that the girl had arrived soon after the incident. It could have been from the cyclist's water bottle bursting on impact, except there was no water bottle here, only a body that bore all the signs of a drowning.

Nothing sensible sprang to Ramsden's mind. There was the sliver of a possibility that someone had knocked the cyclist off his bike, murdered him by forcing litres of liquid down his throat, then ridden away at ten a.m. on a Saturday. But it was a ludicrous notion.

The scenario reminded her of a peculiar incident, years ago, back when she was a desk sergeant. Ramblers stumbled upon the body of twenty-year-old Tyler Carney in Chapel

Field, at the eastern side of the Levels, near the site of the Anglo-Saxon islet of Northeye. Officers found a smoking, burned-out BMW on a track leading to the field, probably stolen by Carney, who they'd collared previously for petty larceny and vandalism. There were bruises on his shoulders but no signs of strangulation or blunt force trauma. The pathologist said he'd drowned. His body wasn't far from the Waller Haven, so it was feasible that someone had dragged him from the water channel after an accident. Trouble was, the liquid in his lungs was briny, which cancelled out the possibility that he had drowned in fresh water. It was the sea that killed him.

The case grew more baffling when a dog walker reported a body in the Pevensey Haven on the same day, a separate channel almost two miles to the west. It was Tyler Carney's girlfriend, Natasha Logan, lain on the riverbank in a fake fur coat, also drowned. The couple were spotted on a train to Eastbourne the previous evening. So what on earth had caused their night to end in tragedy?

One theory was that they went to the Levels to take drugs and became disorientated. Toxicology found small traces of marijuana in their systems, but no class As or alcohol. It was highly unlikely that Tyler and Natasha would go out onto a pitch-black field on a cloudy night just for a few spliffs that they could as easily smoke on the beach, but nobody could piece together a coherent alternative hypothesis. There were no witnesses and no suspects. The case remained unsolved.

'Ma'am!' there was a shout, 'Ma'am!' Sergeant Allsop rounded the corner, huffing and puffing. 'We found the bike.'

'Where?'

'Up a bloody tree about half a mile down the way.'

This brought to Ramsden's mind a peculiar memory from her youth, when she and her best friend stumbled across an upright piano in a field on the Pevensey Levels. It was perfectly intact. A little out of tune, but playable, as if it had been placed there, ready for Elton John to turn up and launch into 'Candle in the Wind'. They bashed out a dodgy version of 'Chopsticks' and fell about laughing. When they returned the following week, the piano had been smashed to tiny pieces in a frenzied attack.

The Levels were so weird.

Another time, they came across a Bible stuck in a hedge. Half the pages had been torn out while every page that remained had been scored with a swastika in what looked like blood.

But this – well, this was something else.

Ramsden looked up at a crow flapping across the wide blue sky. She kept watching until it shrank to a black dot over the Levels. Then she said:

'Okay, so what the hell is going on here, then?'

2. THE STOLEN CAR

It was a friend of their old maths teacher who asked them to steal his car. Up to his eyeballs in debt, he was desperate for a speedy operation on his haemorrhoids. An insurance payout on the theft and destruction of his vintage BMW 2000 would allow him to go private. He reasoned that his teacher friend would know some hooligan who'd nick it for cash, which is how Tyler and Natasha came to be recruited as car thieves.

Tyler had left his wayward teenage ways behind him but couldn't turn down the money. A grand in cash would help them rent a flat in Bexhill. Get them out of their rut and on the way somewhere. The only risky bit was stealing the car from the old codger's house without being noticed. Once they drove onto the Levels, it would be a cinch. There was nobody out there late at night, and by the time anybody spotted the flames, he and Tash would be legging it across the fields, concealed by darkness.

On the train to Eastbourne they kept a low profile, talking quietly. On the way to the house where the BMW was parked they shared a single-skin reefer. Nothing heavy. A mild skunk. They had a car key so they didn't need to smash glass or hot wire the vehicle, though they had instructions to do that when they reached the Levels, to make it look legit.

Natasha was the driver. Tyler's job was to set the thing alight. Trash it good and proper. Besides, Tash was one of those butter-wouldn't-melt types who wouldn't look too suspicious at the wheel of a posh car. She'd even put on one of her mum's fur coats and a ton of makeup to get the right look.

A well crafty move.

The plan was all sorted, they thought, driving out of Eastbourne, through Pevensey, onto the A259, then off the road near Middle Barn Farm. Natasha had already checked it out on Google Maps. There was a convenient dirt track that would take them into a field with some raised ground. They could burn the car on one side and hotfoot it to the nearest lane on the other.

As the car crawled over the mud and stones, they turned off the headlights to stay discreet. Tyler opened the window and leaned out, shining a torch to show Natasha the way ahead. Cold air rushed in, smelling of salt and rotting fish, making them shiver. An uneasy murk enveloped the car, which bucked and swayed on hidden swells and riptides in the mud, like they were being washed downstream. It was hard to tell land from sky, the visible world reduced to an amorphous interplay of densities, shifting and warping as they advanced.

They'd chosen a cloudy night for the theft, but occasionally the moon broke through, shimmering light on flooded ditches and drainage channels, boggy indents and trackways, the imprint of a community long lost. Natasha remembered a geography lesson at school about Nazca lines in Peru. They reminded her of those, and how she thought that the people who left them must have been magicians or aliens. As the clouds reconverged, all traces of light were extinguished but for the beam from Tyler's torch, glancing off the muddy ooze, which swirled and bubbled as if in a deluge, and yet there was no rain.

A trick of the light, Tyler told himself, gritting his teeth. They had to stay focused.

As they turned a bend, his torchlight caught something protruding from a knoll. A human figure, the white of its face caught momentarily in the beam. Eyes like diamonds.

Tyler gasped and shrank back into the vehicle. Natasha slammed the brakes.

'What? What is it, Tyler?'

'I thought I saw someone.'

'You're shitting me.'

'I dunno... I think... it was over there.' Tyler aimed the light at the knoll, but it was just grass and mud, like pretty much everything around here. 'Gone now.'

'You sure?'

'Yeah, sorry. Maybe shouldn't have had that smoke earlier.'

'Don't freak me out, Tyler.' Natasha pushed on the accelerator and the car lurched towards the elevation at the end of the track, a deeper black against the wider blackness, expanding to fill the world as they approached.

They stopped the car and hurried into action. Natasha moved away from the vehicle, while Tyler smashed up the ignition, broke the window and poured a can of petrol over the interior. It was so dark she couldn't see much, but for Tyler's lighter dancing like a will-o'-the-wisp as he removed a twist of rolled-up newspaper and held the flame to it.

'Get further back than that,' said Tyler, 'it's gonna blow.'

Natasha backed off, hugging herself anxiously. Moments later, there was a *whoosh* and shattering glass as flames shot from all sides of the car and the land lit up around them, Tyler a silhouette against the brightness, stumbling to his knees in the aftershock. The hillock behind the burning BMW was now bathed in a red glow. At its crest there was a group of people – maybe five, six or more – in strange woollen clothes, huddled together, looking down at the fire, wide-eyed. Natasha cried out as soon as she saw them. Tyler could see them too. He tried to clamber to his feet, swaying from side to side, as if paralytically drunk.

'Tyler, look out!' cried Natasha as one of the figures began to stride down the hill – a burly, bearded man with tied-back hair and a sheepskin around his shoulders.

Tyler turned to Natasha with a panicked look, but instead of running towards her, he remained rooted to the spot. Confused, he looked down, as if searching for something beneath him. Then he tried to walk towards her, outstretched arms paddling the air, but it was like he was wading through treacle.

He was too slow. Soon, the man was upon him. He span Tyler around, clamped both hands on his shoulders and forced him back down to his knees. Tyler clawed frantically at the man's face, his mouth open in a silent scream, while his attacker glared into his eyes, muttering words that Natasha couldn't make out. For a moment it looked like the two men were locked into an unholy communion rite. A diabolical baptism.

Natasha desperately wanted to run towards them, to stop what was happening, but she felt an invisible liquid force pooling around her. She screamed Tyler's name as a powerful surge tugged her backwards, hoisting her almost completely off the ground, the tips of her toes dragging against the earth as she was swept around the back of the hill, now a rugged black mound framed by fire, growing smaller and fainter as she was pulled and rolled, struggling for breath, turning, turning, turning, until all was darkness.

3. NORTHEYE

They were a community of seven adults and five children, eking out a living on the borderland between earth and water. When the tide went out, they descended the hill with lead pans to extract salt from the briny pools that remained.

It was slow work, but salt was much in demand over in Hoh, that spur of land to the north of their Eyot, where the folk made iron. The rest of their provisions came from strips of reclaimed marshland in which they grew cabbages for the cooking pot and grass for their goats. When the sea rushed in again the surrounding land became a glistening lagoon and they were alone with the warblers and skylarks.

It seemed a peaceful place, but Tedmund lived in fear. Since his grandfather's time, and his grandfather's grandfather's time, the seas encroached with more force each year, taking back much of what they'd claimed. Something had broken down in their discourse with the gods, and the harmony between land and sea was awry. The only way to rebalance the two was to please those gods, which was why Tedmund and his family refused to embrace the Christ cult that had swept into Suth Seaxe. This alien religion might have bent the will of weak-minded folk in Hoh, but not their community. They remained loyal to the old ways, and to Woden, their most powerful god. To abandon him would lead only to destruction.

On clear days, Tedmund could see the ruined fort of Andredceaster in the distance, built by a civilisation long fled from this land, whom his own people had replaced. He was not going to let theirs fall to ruin like that. Tedmund was determined to establish a legacy in this frontier land but he could not understand why the tides were pushing back so vigorously against him. Perhaps it was a message to warn them against conversion to the ways of Christ, or punishment for their acts of reclamation. Tedmund had long feared that their walling and draining innovations had made an enemy of the water dragon they knew as the Knucker. It lived in holes all around Suth Seaxe. If provoked, it could snatch a child in its jaws, lay waste to crops and raze homes to the ground with its fiery breath. Here, it was particularly to be feared, for it could move seamlessly between land and sea, circling their Eyot, hungry for flesh.

Tedmund was certain that the Knucker was lurking out there. Sometimes, when the tide was high, he'd hear an unearthly growl and see wisps of smoke rise from darkening swells, as if a living entity moved beneath the surface.

Should it ever emerge, they would have no choice but to fight and kill it or be killed themselves. The membrane between worlds was thinner out here than the inland-dwelling peoples could ever realise, so Tedmund expected no help with their struggles. It was up to them to stand their ground against malevolent spirits, of which there were many. They'd heard tell that on the Eyot of Horse, on the north-western region of their inland sea, the folk had encountered a 'yellow man', who rode the skeleton of a hunting dog down their hill at terrifying speed. They hurled stones that knocked him headfirst into the waters, where he disappeared beneath the surface as his broken steed span away on the current. Whether an agent of the Knucker or another disturbed spirit, Tedmund knew not, but these were worrying times and they had to remain vigilant.

His wife Bree was wise in the old ways. She made a circle of stones around the Eyot to offer them protection. In a nocturnal high tide, when the spirits were most active, and they were most isolated, she recited her rhymes of banishment. On nights such as those, one of their number was posted as a lookout on a knoll by the lagoon's edge.

As fate would have it, Sigeweard stood on guard when the Knucker finally came.

Hours after sunset, a freakishly rapid tide sent water shooting through channels and pooling in syrupy whirls around their Eyot. Sigeweard was an elder of the community and used to the vagaries of the sea, but he knew instantly that something was amiss. A rasping sound emanated from the south, and two eyes, bright as moons, pierced the night. He whistled to alert Tedmund and the others, then stood his ground as a black shape cut through the water, a solitary eye flashing. He could hear its belly rumble and a deep growling noise as it grew closer. When its glowering eye lit upon his face, he fell backwards in surprise, scrabbling away from the knoll on hands and knees.

It was the Knucker for sure. Sigeweard prayed to Woden that Tedmund had raised the adults from their slumber, for the beast was coming.

Tedmund was indeed awake. He stood outside his hut with Bree, Oswine, Tata, Aedelstan and Hildred, their children safely inside. Even in the darkness, they could see the flashing eye of the Knucker and its hard black skin glimmer in shards of moonlight. They watched in horror as it proceeded, slowly but surely, towards their Eyot, water swelling around its bulk. Then it stopped, suddenly, and its growling fell silent, as if it was waiting to pounce. Bree gripped Tedmund's arm.

'I shall defend you,' he said, as best he could, for his heart thumped with terror. They were lowly folk, without weapons and with only their gods to protect them. That is, if they hadn't been forsaken.

Without warning, the dragon blasted fire across the water, lighting up their Eyot, exposing them on the slope. In the glare they saw a human form, an emissary of the beast, rise up from the water until he was waist deep, his arms paddling against the current.

Tedmund knew he must act while the enemy was vulnerable. He strode down the hill, gripped the spirit's shoulders, and forced him downward until his bony white head was beneath the surface, bubbles streaming from his open mouth. The Knucker roared with angry flame but Tedmund persisted, pledging oaths to Woden should he die in this moment.

A shrieking voice assailed him across the lagoon with a cry of 'Tyler!' and he could see in the distance a furry beast, part human, part animal, rising from the surf. But he did not let it sway him. He held that spirit down and kept on holding until there was no more resistance.

Eventually, the Knucker's flame was extinguished and the night fell silent around Tedmund, but for the lapping of water as it kissed the land he called home.

4. HORSE EYE

Greg was making good time and felt fit, but damn it was hot. He'd started his cycle ride at eight a.m. to beat this infernal sun. To no avail. The sky was cloudless, air still, and by the time he reached the Pevensey Levels, the land was hard-baked.

Sweat soaked Greg's yellow Lycra top as he rode at speed down the twisting B-road from Herstmonceux, huffing and puffing, the hedgerows blurring either side of him, his ears alert for the sound of approaching cars. But it was a quiet

Saturday morning. The roads were empty and the world felt like his domain.

At Horse Eye his legs worked harder, adjusting to the incline that lifted him up over the Levels. At its crest he marvelled at the mirage before him, for it seemed as if the fields as far as Pevensey Castle had been submerged by the sea, with treetops protruding from the waves. Water, water everywhere. But that simply could not be.

As Greg's bicycle dipped into the downward slope he was surprised by an outburst of commotion in the adjacent field. A group of people in strange woollen clothes ran towards him, clutching rocks, angry and shouting.

MY FATHER, THE MOTORWAY BRIDGE

Have you met my father?

He's the final bridge before junction 12 on the M25. You cannot miss him. Dad spans all six lanes, so it doesn't matter which direction you drive.

At first, you'll see two twenty-metre concrete towers, bulbous at the top. Like sewing needles. Except much bigger than sewing needles – I mean, really massive. Then, as you get closer, you'll notice suspension wires connected to a horizontal deck.

Normally, bridges go straight over a road in the shortest way possible. But my father skews diagonally across the motorway, the way you slice a baguette to make garlic bread.

That's Dad for you. A true one-off.

Now, you might well snigger at that. One-off? *Really*?

Hey-ho. Whatever. No skin off my nose. You wouldn't be the first to react in that way. Like most people, you assume that all motorway bridges are pretty much the same and not worth special consideration.

Wrong!

Go back and read my description again. Think about it for a few minutes. Picture it in your head. Now tell me that you've seen a bridge exactly like that.

Bet you can't.

Anyway, I expect you're thinking of motorway bridges that carry roads. Single lanes. Dual carriageways. Access roads. That kind of thing. Occasionally, you see cows walking over them. Or a lonely man staring down. Or a rozzer with a speed camera. Dad's not one of those. He's a railway bridge, which is far less common. And not any railway bridge either, but the first all-concrete cable stayed railway bridge in the world.

Beat that!

My father is a proper *first*, like Neil Armstrong or Sir Edmund Hillary. But growing up in his shadow isn't as hard as you'd think. After all, there's not much pressure to better your dad's achievements when you're a human being and he's a fifty-five-metre bridge.

Sometimes I wish a kid had come up to me at school and said, 'Thea Stanton, is your dad *really* the first concrete cable stayed railway bridge in the world?'

But that never happened.

See, the problem with Dad being a railway bridge is that most people don't think of him as a railway bridge at all. That sounds strange but think about it. When you're driving on a motorway and you see a bridge, you tend to think, 'Motorway bridge!' You don't adapt your terminology to suit what's going over that bridge. If it's a railway bridge, you still think 'motorway bridge', because it's going over a motorway. But when you see a railway bridge in a town, you don't think 'road bridge' because it's going over a road.

Weird that, isn't it?

So while my father is, technically, the Lyne Railway Bridge, you'd probably know him as a motorway bridge.

Fine by me. I just think, *that's my father*. Good old Dad. Solid and reliable. Always there for me, wind, rain or shine. Those qualities are at the core of his being and will never change, no matter what happens to me. No matter how many more tragedies strike our family. No matter how much time I spend in hospital.

They're what make him *him*.

And, by default, they're what makes me *me*.

I've always looked up to Dad. Ever since I was little. Though truth be told, most people look up to him. You'd need to be a giant or a helicopter pilot to look down on him. And how many people are those things? Hardly any.

If you've been on the M25 orbital, you've looked up to him too, even if you weren't conscious of it. Maybe you were singing along to your stereo or having an argument with the person in the passenger seat. Even so, your eyes will have seen him. Your brain will have processed the signals your eyes sent up your optical nerve. Like it or not, Dad will be in your head, deep in one of the cortexes (I'd have to google which one, sorry). As you pass under him, the light changes for a moment as he casts a line of shadow over you, like an airport scanner going over a bag. So you sense my father's presence, even if your busy mind ignores that feeling.

That's why you could ask a bunch of people, 'Do you know Thea Stanton's dad, the world's first all-concrete cable stayed railway bridge?' And they'd all say, 'No!' (well, maybe apart from one weird guy with a beard and glasses).

But, actually, they do know my father. They just don't realise it.

And that guy with the beard and glasses? He'll be one of those curious types who do notice motorway bridges. If anything, they *over-notice* them, to the point that they get quite het up about the ones they don't like. Take, for instance, the man on an online forum who wrote:

> It's the design of those towers that ruins it for me.
> Specifically, the way they get wider and more
> blocky towards the top. It makes them look
> top-heavy and unwieldy.
> There's no grace about them whatsoever.

Pah! Well of course Dad isn't graceful. He's tall and strong. He needs to be so that he can hold himself together with those high-tension wires. You try being graceful with a bloody great train on your back!

Thankfully, not everyone thinks like that.

There is a woman up in Manchester who painted a portrait of my father and put it in an exhibition. She paints lots of motorway bridges and says that Dad's the one who means the most to her. I don't feel jealous. Only proud.

Her painting is a bit fuzzy, more like a memory of the bridge than the bridge itself. There are no cars in the painting. But that's the thing. Who remembers cars? When you think about the bridge, it's all about the towers and wires, and the way the bridge makes you feel. That's what people remember.

Looking at that empty motorway, it's just me and Dad. The two of us together. Which is how I like it to be.

That said, he looks a bit different to how he appears in that painting. My father changes over the years, when the council paint him or graffiti artists daub stuff on him. For instance, at the moment, he bears the word HELCH. I don't know what it means. He doesn't know what it means. But he wears it with dignity. Even when exhaust fumes turn him black and birds shit on him, Dad stays strong and does his job.

He's a motorway bridge and he knows it.

It sometimes makes me sad, when I see other people out and about with their dads, while mine must always remain where he is, straddling the M25. I cannot invite him to the hospital for my eighteenth birthday. I cannot watch a terrible, cringey TV show like *Hollyoaks* with him. I cannot hug him and tell him about my cancer.

I cannot and will not. Because he's a motorway bridge, you see? D'uh!

It's not the done thing to move a bridge to a hospital. Totally impractical. You'd have to lift Dad up with a crane and put him onto a truck, then drive him around like King Kong, humiliated.

If that happened, would he still even be a bridge?

That's the thing about bridges. They are bridges when

they bridge, but when they don't bridge they become something else. And I don't want to lose my father. Not again.

Instead of him coming to my ward to see me, I wish I could get up on one of his towers. He could hold me aloft like a child at a rock concert and we could look out over the motorway we know so well. It's our bit of road and it means everything to us.

Ever since I was born, I travelled along this stretch of the M25 over and over. That's because Grandma and Granddad lived in Bracknell, while we lived in Crawley. So we'd be up and down to their house all the time, taking the turn-off at junction 12. Quite often the M25 was slow or congested. Long, boring tailbacks that seemed to never end.

'Are we nearly there yet?' I'd moan from the back seat.

'Wait for it, Thea,' Dad would say, trying to stop me bursting into tears. 'Wait until you see the big fat pillars of that bridge. It means we're nearly there, nearly there.'

When the bridge eventually appeared in the distance, Dad would yell: 'There she blows! Time to turn off! Time to turn to turn off!'

He did it every single time without fail. Like clockwork. Until it would have been really weird for him *not* to say, 'There she blows! Time to turn off!'

I guess it's a dad thing.

That's all I remember of him, at four years old. It's the only piece of him that lodged in my silly young brain. By the time I turned five, he was gone.

Dead. Just like that.

When I was growing up, all that remained of Dad in my brain was that memory of the bridge. Its towers. The suspension wires. The shadow slicing across us as we passed beneath, and his voice saying, 'Time to turn off.'

Time to turn off.

To turn off time.

To make time hard like concrete.

To hold that time tight with suspension wires.

To never let it go, the memory of the bridge and Dad. The bridge and Dad. The bridge and Dad. The bridge and Dad.

The bridge Dad.

The Dad bridge.

I would plead with Mum to drive under him, weekend after weekend, month after month, year after year, until I become too ill to leave hospital. But even here, among these machines, white walls and worried faces, I can check on Google Maps and see that he's there, solid and dependable, as always.

My rock.

My everything.

My father, the motorway bridge.

BIN DAY

FOUR DAYS BEFORE BIN DAY

It is only Monday and already I'm thinking about bin day.

The stress is almost unbearable. There are so many uncertainties, it brings me out in a sweat. I might miss the collection by sleeping in too late. My household rubbish might be ignored or my recycling rejected, for god knows what reason, so elusive are their criteria. You need a degree in materials science to differentiate between the forms of plastic; to understand what's permitted or disallowed. Then there's the danger that gulls and foxes will savage the bags and leave my refuse strewn outside my house, so that everyone can see my discarded beer cans, ready meals for one and leftover meat, stinking in the sun.

No matter what I do to distract myself, bin day lurks at the edges of my waking thoughts, haunting me with its imminence.

I wonder if anybody else feels this way?

I cannot believe so, otherwise more people would be up in arms about it. Organising protests. Signing petitions. Demanding to speak to their MP. The whole street would be talking about bin day. Not that I bother listening to my neighbours, with their lies and accusations. As if I'd kill cats and foxes then leave them in my backyard to go rotten.

What nonsense.

They're a worse class of people here in Ramsgate. Not like in Hampstead, where Linda and I spent most of our married life. We liked our neighbours there. They looked out for you.

How's your day going, Steve? They would say to me. I've got an Amazon parcel for you, Steve. Love the new Audi, Steve, very nice.

They were the sort who could afford five-bedroom houses in London. I'm not a snob but it goes without saying that a higher property price threshold sorts the wheat from the chaff when it comes to neighbour quality.

That was a wonderful house. Big front garden. Room for two wheelie bins by the viburnum hedge, accessible by dustbin men without any need to drag them into place on the big day. We could consume as much as we wanted and chuck all the waste in the wheelie bin. When it became full, the second bin was backup. Linda and I could go to Edinburgh or Paris for a break, then return to find the bins empty. Clean as a whistle. No litter all over the road. They had a machine that tilted the bins directly into the van.

Ruthlessly efficient it was in Hampstead, back then.

Recycling was easier, too. There was a tub for food waste and they gave us spacious colour-coded boxes so that we could toss in the plastic and paper, and never think about it again.

Saying that, I've always been sceptical about recycling. My old mate Ollie says it's a scam and they shove it all in a hole with the usual garbage. Pile earth over it. Pocket the government's money and ride the hell out of that gravy train under the guise of 'global warming'.

Still, I'm a man who plays by the rules. If there's a system, I follow it. Cannot help myself. I've got a thing for order. It's a quality of mine that got up Linda's nose eventually, after the first decade of marriage, but that's marriage, isn't it? A breeding ground for animosity. Watching her stack the dishwasher was a horror show. Bowls and plates tilted into each other. Cutlery dangling through holes in the tray so that the blades jammed and the crockery came out crusty. Linda could see what the system was – what room there was in the machine and what slots were allocated for each item – but she didn't care.

Linda, you bitch, I'd yell, raising the hammer up high in my trembling fist, that's not how things are done!

But you know, there were some good times, back then, before that bloody virus disrupted everything. She was earning a fortune from her consultancy job and I was doing okay with a little freelance accounting. We had what we needed. A car, nice house, pleasant neighbours, excellent bins, and a collection system which worked very well.

It's not like that now. Not in this town. They make it hard for a man like me. Very hard indeed. There's no space for a wheelie bin outside these Victorian workers' cottages. Instead, they provide an industrial sack which you're supposed to hook on your railing. There's enough room inside for about two small bin bags. That's it.

You want to put more rubbish in? Tough luck. You can't.

Instead, those extra bags lie out in the open air, totally exposed, where they are torn to shreds by foxes or herring gulls. Even inside the sack, your refuse is accessible to any animal with enough tenacity. All your waste ends up on the street the next morning so that your neighbours can judge you. Make accusations. Call the police. Whatever.

Same goes for the recycling. You can forget about plastic containers. I have to put all my recycling in a council-issue pink polythene bag with *Get it Sorted!* written on it. Use anything else and they won't pick it up. I once put my recycling into a black bin liner but wrote the words *RECYCLING – PLEASE TAKE, COUNCIL OVERLORDS!* on a massive carboard tag, yet they ignored it. You must use their silly bags or be damned. Which means that next-door's vegan hippies can tut at my empty tins of Heinz beans and sausages.

What a shitshow.

I rue the day Linda made us move here. It was all her fault. I don't even believe she had Covid anxiety, as she claimed. She just didn't know how to transfer her consultancy work online. Couldn't handle the technology. Got ideas in her head about connecting with nature. Wanted to flee the capital and come to the coast for a fresh start. Although I would never use the word 'fresh' here. Flyblown, maybe, but never fresh, not with the bin situation the travesty that it is.

The day we moved here was the day it all went wrong for us. Perhaps that was Linda's plan all along. Drag our marriage to the coastline and let it rot, picked apart by feral beasts until it was nothing but bleached bones. Instead of going out every day to earn money like she used to, she stayed indoors, tormenting me with blithering diatribes about mindfulness until my ears could not take another word, not another bloody word.

Well, it worked, Linda. Consider me tormented, Linda. And now you've gone, my mindful Linda, leaving me to deal with bin day all alone.

THREE DAYS BEFORE BIN DAY

This heatwave has been going on for two months. I've never known anything like it. You can't leave your bin bag out in this kind of heat. It reeks! Sure, it might be alright for the vegans next door with their potato peelings and pumpkin seeds, but I've been throwing away meat. There's no way I'm putting that into a sack outside my front door. It's just not right. May as well lay out a smorgasbord of snacks for the local pests and let them come from miles around.

Neither can I risk stinking out my backyard, not since the incident with the dead cat, or the neighbours will start having a go at me again. This is why I've been storing perishable rubbish in a chest freezer in the outhouse in my yard until bin day. Stops the smell. Keeps it from going off. Avoids predation by beasts.

I bought the freezer second hand, using money I cannot afford to spend – not until I can access that house sale money in Linda's bank account – and all because I got sick of foxes, cats and gulls poking around the bin bags that I left in my backyard after I missed a catastrophic two collections in a row.

I still shudder to think about it.

I missed the first one because I had gone on a trip to visit my sister after the lockdown ended, and the second because I slept in, so I didn't get my rubbish out in time. It meant I had several sacks of waste in the back going funky in the relentless bloody sunshine. My yard became a feeding ground for scavengers and, yes, unfortunately, one of the cats did die. Not from my doing but from its own incompetence, getting stuck in the outhouse and sweltering to death. I assumed the stink was from the rubbish, which was why I never noticed.

One day the neighbour, Phil – an absolute bellend, I have to say – was poking his bald head over the fence, asking the whereabouts of his cat and wondering if I could check the shed. Then his wife – don't know her name to be honest with you – stuck her big face up next to his, so they were like Punch and Judy, bleating on about how they were sorry for the trouble but they were distressed about their cat and concerned about the smell coming from my yard. They didn't have much sympathy with my refuse problems and kept nagging me until I was forced to open the outhouse door in a huff. It was a bit stiff, so I gave it a yank, then all these bluebottles came rushing at me.

Phil and his big-faced wife cried out before I even saw the cat lying there, dehydrated, legs stiff.

Stupid creature.

Anyway, if that's what happens when there's a dead cat in my yard, the neighbours are going to become suspicious again when my perishables start going off. So now I parcel them up in cellophane and put them in the freezer. When it's bin day, I transfer the contents to a black bag, then get it onto the road. This is not something I can do the night before, because foxes feast when it's dark, nor in the early hours of the morning, as that's when the birds descend. It's hatching season right now. Every chimney in town has a gull, fat on the rubbish it steals from unprotected bins.

Thing is, while the neighbours carry out their whispering campaign against me because of the dead cat, and that fox they said I killed with a brick, they refuse to acknowledge the effort I make to contain my rubbish in a sanitary way that doesn't encourage vermin. Aside from spaffing cash on a freezer, I bought a new wheelie bin to put outside my bay window so I could store rubbish in there instead of those idiotic sacks. But some snake in the grass complained. A woman from the council rang up and told me that the bin men were not allowed to extract bags from an unauthorised wheelie bin. Besides, she said, it was jutting onto the pavement, causing an obstruction to pedestrians. She was sorry, but I would have to return to the sanctioned sack system.

I said to her, look, love, your sack system is a disgrace. All it does is leave a trail of devastation. There's a godawful pong all summer, I said, which didn't happen when I was in London. She replied, Well you're not in London any more are you?

The bloody cheek.

No, I said, I am in a kind of hell called Ramsgate, watching other people's crisp packets roll down the street like tumbleweed.

Well, she said, in a quite high-handed manner, that's the system we have here, which snookered me because, as you know, I'm a sucker for a system. This is why, under great duress, I have introduced a combination of freezer technology and an alarm clock to ensure that what I throw away gets taken away.

Good riddance to bad rubbish, as they say. Haha!

TWO DAYS BEFORE BIN DAY

Well, this is a right load of arse. Looking in my chest freezer, I see that there's too much organic matter for the two bin bags I can fit in the council-approved sack. An obvious solution is to shove it in the back of a car and drive to a tip, but after I got banned for drink-driving Linda said that we couldn't afford to a car any more, and besides, it was unethical to pollute the air for the sake of our convenience, so that was that.

Silly cow.

Linda and I never got round to kids. She wanted a career and I didn't want toddlers coating our house in piss and shit. So I don't have some strapping lad I can call to help his dad take some refuse to the tip, and there's nobody with whom I am on good enough terms to ask for a loan of their car.

That said, it's too risky to get other people involved in bin day, so I'm extracting the waste in incremental stages. I put some of the stuff from the freezer into the black bag collection last week, and from the looks of things, I have another two bin days before it's completely gone. So I cannot even breathe a sigh of relief on Friday afternoon and kick back with a few Stellas, because the process is not over, not by a long shot.

This is what I mean when I say unbearable stress. I'm not only thinking about this bin day, but two more bin days after that.

To add to the pressure, this heatwave shows no sign of ending. It's worse than the one last year. I'd get panicky about the environmental causes, like Linda used to, but I read online that actually the ice caps are gaining more snow, contrary to what scientists have been saying, so I am not about to become another sheep, mindlessly nodding along to the green agenda, while they remove all of our liberties. I'm a thinker, not a doer, as Linda herself told me, albeit with an unpleasant look on her face.

Make no mistake, I'm all for being efficient and keeping things clean, so I'm naturally environmentally friendly. I don't need to virtue signal about it. But Linda droned on endlessly about her ecological awakening after we moved to the coast, as if we were going to save the world simply by not living in London. She was always trying to impress the hippy family by saying things like: Oh, the big city became too much during the lockdowns and we wanted to simplify our lives and get back to basics. Reduce our carbon footprint. Care less about business and money. Ha. As if that was the real reason and not because she bottled her job because – well, I don't know why, something to do with reading too much lefty middle-class guilt bollocks in *The Guardian*.

Linda didn't realise how ridiculous she looked, a fifty-two-year-old woman becoming woke at the cost of everything we held dear. Our home. Our friends. Our car. Our front garden with its massive wheelie bins.

You're wrong about man-made climate change, darling, I'd say, holding her throat tightly, feeling the sinews twist beneath my fingertips. You're playing right into the hands of global elites who want to install a dictatorship.

I don't know if I fully believed that or not, but it was nice to see her eyes bulge.

THE DAY BEFORE BIN DAY

What a disaster. My worst nightmare.

On the eve of bin day, somebody has stolen my council-issue sack. When I went out this morning to get milk from the corner shop, it was no longer hanging from the railing outside my door.

I'm wracking my brains to figure out how this could have happened.

About six months ago, it blew away in a storm, so I was forced to steal one from the senile old lady's house down the road. But last night had been calm and windless. Deathly still. Which could only mean that this was sabotage. Someone probing my weak point. Trying to get at me the best way they know how – through my bin. Maybe it was the hippy kids next door, the ones who think I'm killing all the baby gulls, or Phil and his wife getting me back for the cat.

Whatever the reason, I am now in a state of total binlessness.

This has raised the stakes significantly. Anything I put outside will have zero protection from the scavenging monsters of Ramsgate. And by that I mean foxes, cats and gulls, not the neighbours, hahahaha. Although who knows if there is a difference any more? Humans and beasts alike prowl around my front door at night, meddling with my property, interfering with the order of things.

Trouble is, I cannot phone the council to get another sack delivered because there has been some kind of block on my phone number, ever since I took up a campaign of daily calls regarding my grievance over missed collections and how wheelie bins would end the horror of their sack-based system.

I have no regrets. If the community won't act in its own interest then I shall take on the burden of responsibility and get something done, even if it means I am scorned and shunned for it. There was another, more famous man who underwent a similar ordeal, nailed to a cross on Calvary Hill, and we all know how that turned out.

I shall let history judge my deeds.

Anyway, whenever I phone them, the council now leave me on hold or an intern passes me from pillar to post until I'm forced to give up. It's an outrage. I pay my taxes. I'm a qualified accountant from a middle-class background, not some dole-bothering scumbag. My wife was a highly regarded marketing consultant whose advice helped hundreds of small businesses flourish, boosting the British economy. She was even interviewed in a magazine. Though truth be told, her success was a great deal down to me allowing her to take the more dominant work role, while I selflessly put my accountancy dreams to one side and ran the household. She could barely fill a dishwasher, never mind deal with something as complex as bin day.

The only talent you have, I told her, arm locked behind her back, pushing her against the sink, forcing her peroxide blonde head down towards the foaming dishwater, is teaching people marketing strategies, while I have to multitask using a myriad different skills for a myriad different tasks, both physical and mental. Yet you're the one featured in a magazine. You're the one getting fawned over on Twitter. You're the one the neighbours want to talk to. You make me sick.

Thing is, I am right, even if it's not politically correct to say it. The world has gone wilfully blind at the command of a vocal minority. Nobody sees the guy like me, busy below deck, keeping the engine room running. I am one of those men who stepped aside so that women could fulfil their insatiable ambition for power, only to find that when it came to the crunch, my wife didn't want the responsibility. All our hopes thrown away. Yet it's me who the council consider a pariah and a drain on resources.

It's maddening because I really don't want this hassle in my life right now. I don't want to have to ring up officials and then have them snooping around, poking their noses into my business. I only want a quiet life, and for that to happen I really need these next few bin days to go without a hitch. There are items in my freezer which urgently need to go into the dustbin vans and get taken far, far away from here. It's all packed in where there should be bags of peas and oven chips, so the situation is not ideal. Not ideal whatsoever.

There's alarming information on the news about the damage that the freakishly hot weather is doing to the country's infrastructure.

Bridges and dams cracking.

Railway lines warping.

Flash floods.

They're saying the system cannot take it. That we're on the precipice. It's beginning to worry me. I live in fear that a power cut from a natural disaster might result in the freezer switching off for days on end. The stench of decay will waft from my yard like an olfactory distress flare, bringing all and sundry to my doorstep, asking me inconvenient questions for which there are no easy answers.

BIN DAY!

I had a torrid, sleepless night. The humidity was unbearable. It's like living in the tropics these days. I had the bedroom window wide open, but all I could hear was the sound of the TV blaring from the house of the deaf sod across the road, blended with the shrieks and barks of rutting foxes.

A right hullabaloo.

By the time I finally managed to fall asleep, the evil gulls commenced their dawn chorus, cackling in spirals above the rooftops, waking me up again.

Lying amidst all that clamour at five a.m., I wondered if it would be easier if I just got up, made coffee, and started packing the bin bags. I had switched off the freezer late last night to allow a bit of defrosting, otherwise the rock-hard, blockish contents of my bin bags might arouse suspicion. From my observations these past weeks, the bin men rarely consider the contents of bags. They just pick them out of the sack, or directly off the street, and hurl them into the truck. However, I don't want to give them any reason to consider that I might be throwing away something which is non-regulation. Which is why I need the meatier packages to have a bit of natural give.

It was while I was mulling over these issues that I fell into a deep, exhausted slumber from which even my alarm, set accidentally at a feeble volume, could not arouse me at eight a.m.

Now I am awake! And what is that I can hear? Crunching plastic! The shouts and calls of binmen! The chunter of a large engine!

Can it be that time already?

Oh my god, no.

In a panic, I tumble out of bed and run downstairs in nothing but my underpants, skittering into the backyard and pulling open the door of the outhouse. There is soupy brown water seeping from the defrosting freezer, flooding the concrete floor.

I fling open the freezer lid and heave the cellophane-wrapped packages into bin liners, swearing profusely. The beaks of some of the herring gulls are poking through the wrapping like yellow hooks and there's blood trickling from some of the packages, but there isn't time to worry about that right now.

I fill the first bag, half with the freezer meat, half with general waste from my kitchen bin. Then I run outside and dump it on the doorstep, glancing up nervously for circling birds. I can see the dustbin lorry grind to a stop about five houses down. With time running out, I return to my yard and pull out some of the heavier, more problematic meat waste. I load as much as I can into the second bin liner, along with what's left of my general kitchen refuse, just as air brakes hiss outside the front door.

They are here. I need to move fast.

I haul the bin bag down the hall and onto my doorstep, panting heavily. To my horror, there is a bin man approaching to my right just as, to my left, Phil's big-faced wife emerges from their front door.

She turns to me with a look of distaste as I launch forward to hand the man my bin bag. I feel a tug when the bag snags on the railing spike, but there is nothing I can do. Momentum carries me forward while the torn black polythene yawns open and its contents spill onto the pavement. Semi-frozen blocks of unwanted meat thwack onto the slabs, sending up tiny jets of red spray, among eggshells, burnt toast and bloodied rags.

Standing there in my underpants, on what might turn out to be my final bin day, I despair at what – in the light of a bright Friday morning – is clearly not regulation refuse. Even beneath all the wrapping you can see the flesh and sinew.

Despite the sheer awfulness of the moment, I have a perverse notion that I should turn to Phil's big-faced wife and say, Well it looks like the cat is now literally out of the bag. But I think twice about that, as the matted peroxide blonde hair bristling through a tear in the cellophane is obviously not that of a cat, nor a fox, although there are plenty of those in the other bin bag, should anyone want to take a peek, and they probably will now, worst luck, things being how they are.

The meat might be defrosting but time has frozen in this excruciating moment. As we stand there – me, the dustbin man and Phil's big-faced wife – staring at my unspeakable waste, we enter a hell in which the only reality is bin day, stretched out for an eternity, and all the joys of man are but a fleeting dream.

MEET ON THE EDGE

The morning air felt curiously thin, as if Melissa had ascended a mountain instead of clambering into the driver's seat of her SUV. She felt a little dizzy. Maybe it was nerves or something. Silly really. She wasn't doing anything wrong. Melissa breathed deeply. Once. Twice. *Good*. Then she fired up the engine and drove out of town, occasionally checking herself out in the sun visor mirror, humming a half-remembered Nine Inch Nails tune.

A congested single lane took her to the interchange beneath a crisscross of flyovers. After a crawl through traffic lights, she hit the dual carriageway, whizzing past car showrooms and high-rise office blocks until she spotted the rectangle obelisk of the retail park sign silhouetted against the blue sky.

B&Q was already busy. Bald-headed men emerged through the sliding doors, pushing platform trolleys stacked with merchandise. Melissa circled the mass of stationary vehicles until she reached the car park's perimeter, where a verge of bark chippings met a box hedge. Here the white lines of the parking bays were faded and scorched with rubber from nocturnal wheelspins, the kerb littered with crushed cans, cigarette butts and sun-bleached crisp packets.

In this B&Q hinterland, there were relatively few cars. Not only was it the area furthest away from the store, but it was on the other side of a strip of pine trees, bordered by a wooden fence, which jutted into the car park, rendering the store as a patchwork of orange fragments among the foliage. It was the parking zone of last resort. But even if it filled up, Melissa supposed nobody would pay much attention to her. People were here to buy power tools and lawnmowers, tiles and flooring, paint and wallpaper paste. The car park was nothing more than a tarmac sea, to be crossed as quickly as possible. She watched shoppers hurry from their vehicles as she bit her nails, hoping that Letitia would appear, as promised.

Melissa had first bumped into Letitia the previous Saturday morning. Sick of being stuck in the house, she'd volunteered to buy paint for her eldest's bedroom. Axel wanted black walls, inspired by his discovery of her old Placebo CDs. She was pleased that he was crate-digging her teenage music collection – but black? No, no, no. Her in-laws stayed in his bedroom at Christmas. Black wasn't conducive to a harmonious visit. 'It's very gloomy in here, Melissa.' 'Is Axel on drugs, Melissa?' That kind of thing. Neither would black fit with the sophisticated neutrals from Farrow & Ball throughout the rest of her house. Besides,

Axel was one of those kids who went through phases faster than pints of milk. No doubt he'd be a hippy in a month's time when he discovered her Kula Shaker CDs and they'd have to paint his room again. So Melissa encouraged him to choose grey, to match his bed frame. To get the hues right, she opted for B&Q's colour matching service. The paint needed mixing by the lad with the buzzcut who manned the counter. Once he'd blended the colours, he slid the pot into a Valspar paint machine and pressed a button. The mixer juddered so hard that the counter shook. Melissa heard guffawing and turned to see a plump woman in a tie-dye top and blue jeans, sporting an astonishing number of bangles on one wrist and rings on every finger.

'I love this bit!' Letitia cried. 'Gotta get me one of these for home, wink wink.' She nudged Melissa so roughly that she almost fell over.

The more the machine juddered, the more Letitia laughed, setting off the lad behind the desk, who also began to laugh. Suddenly Melissa was at it too, HA HA HA HA HA, she couldn't help herself. HA HA HA HA HA HA. She laughed her guts out, folded over, holding onto the counter. HA HA HA HA HA.

It felt like an exorcism. All the months of stress over work, the arguments with Matty about the kids and who wasn't pulling their weight with the cleaning and shopping and childcare. It all came roaring out of her.

'You alright?' said Letitia.

'Christ no,' said Melissa.

'Come here often?'

It was what a bloke might have asked Melissa at a pub, back when she could freely go to that kind of place. It sounded so funny here with the sawdust smell and pot-bellied men bumbling around with trollies full of U-bends, brushes and beading.

'I come here as little as possible,' said Melissa. 'And you?'

'Can't keep me away. I've got a thing about paint machines.'

They talked for a while about the weather and how the disruptive roadworks in town were taking far too long to complete. Neither of them cared about the roadworks, nor the weather. But it distracted them from the raucous drum 'n' bass of the paint mixer. And ten minutes later, when they bumped into each other again at the checkout, they laughed once more, this time for no obvious reason at all.

As Melissa returned to her car, Letitia followed, both swinging tins of paint by their sides, chatting breezily. It turned out they were parked near each other. Letitia said that her van was on the other side of the dented shipping container which had been dumped on the perimeter. Melissa laughed at the idea of her driving a white van, like some kind of catcalling builder.

'Don't be so prejudiced!' cackled Letitia. 'I'm doing good work busting clichés here. Not like you with your people carrier. Just how many people do you *have*, girl?'

'I'll happily swap. Then you can go home and feed my kids tonight!'

Their banter felt so comfortable, Melissa didn't want it to stop. She was overcome with a compulsion to ask Letitia inside the car to chat for a while. Anything to delay the drive home. She hadn't talked in confidence to another soul outside of her family for so long it felt thrilling to sit with a stranger, especially this one. Letitia had an infectious warmth and piercing eyes – stark black rings around green irises that seemed to whirl as she smiled. Those eyes remained fixed on Melissa, with barely a blink, which was disconcerting at first, but soon became comforting, as if they were somehow pulling her closer.

Melissa was unable to resist. As she started to speak, feelings tumbled out which she had never consciously formulated into words. She told Letitia that she was sick of the life in which she'd ended up, surrounded by flatpack furniture, pasta machines and Nigella Lawson cookbooks, enslaved by sulky children and ignored by a husband whose only remaining passions were football and Rachel Riley from *Countdown*.

It hadn't always been like this. Before she met Matty she'd enjoyed a misspent youth of mascara, speed and ear-bleedingly loud rock music. Now she had found herself parked somewhere she had never meant to stop. Marriage and two kids had scrubbed out any expectation that anything genuinely new could happen. Nothing of significance, anyway. Nothing that would redefine her. It was as if time had stalled and the future had vanished. Every day was another circling of the same airspace.

Letitia listened eagerly. She nodded at the right times and made the right noises –'ummm' and 'ahhh,' and 'oh yes' – consuming Melissa's troubles like a fine wine. At the end of the confession she said, 'This can happen in life. But we all have the power to change.'

She told Melissa about how she used to be a junior building surveyor but grew weary of valuing properties she could not afford herself. When the pandemic struck, she was furloughed. With extra time on her hands, she started decorating the house she shared and discovered a real knack for it. After restrictions eased, she would do up her friends' and neighbours' homes at the weekends for cash. Soon she was getting enough work through word of mouth to cover her rent. That was when she abandoned her career.

'None of it seemed important any more, what with the world going to hell. People dying. Racists on the streets. Bigots in my office. Fuck that. I'd rather fix things up. Hammers and nails, glues and paints. In all the madness they're things I can control. I use them to make something beautiful. For me, each day is a fresh canvas.'

'I'm so envious. Do you know that before I came into the store today I parked up and sat for a while? Just because I was out of the house. Just because I could. How sad is that?'

'Oh, I saw you,' said Letitia. 'As I came out of the van this morning, I saw you well enough. I see lots of you out here, sitting alone.'

'Is that why you talked to me – back at the paint counter? You felt sorry for me?'

'Nah, course not. I like to listen, that's all. It feeds my soul.' Her eyes narrowed. 'You know what I mean?'

Letitia wanted a cigarette, so they stood on the verge behind the SUV, like girls on a school trip. Melissa cadged the occasional puff, enjoying the head rush. Must have been fifteen years since she smoked a fag. The feel of a cigarette on her lips, it was like hurtling through a time portal. She had a sudden craving for a can of lager. That metallic tinge you only get from drinking a tinny outdoors.

The taste of youth.

'I miss this,' she told Letitia. 'Not the nicotine. Just the not-giving-a-shit.'

Ever since she settled down to marriage, career and kids, Melissa ditched the drugs, pubs and gigging and tried to do the right thing. Being a good team leader at work, even when most days she didn't care because she knew, deep down, that the company didn't care about her. Chatting with mums at the school gates, pretending to enjoy their gossip. Making costumes for World Book Day, even though she could barely sew on a button. Hosting dinner parties, replete with scallop entrées and chocolate fondants, at which she never allowed herself to tell the wicked jokes that popped into her brain or dared challenge the anodyne generalisations of the braying men who dominated conversations. She kept her unruly edges hidden so that she could be the kind of person that everyone got on with. Yet she doubted anybody really knew anything about her beyond the generic working mum schtick she'd been so desperate to uphold.

During the coronavirus pandemic, few bothered to get in touch, or invite her to their Zoom chats. After the restrictions began to lift, what little social life she had was nothing more than a series of 'likes' and comments on other people's Facebook posts. She told Letitia that she doubted anyone outside her family would bother much if she vanished suddenly. They'd make some consoling noises to Matty, but it wouldn't make much difference to them. It wouldn't leave a hole.

'You are not a hole, girl,' said Letitia. 'You're a whole girl, do you get me?'

Melissa laughed. 'Thanks.'

'I'm serious. I'm getting something from you, and it isn't nothing.'

Afterwards, Melissa and Letitia both agreed that it had been good to talk. To get things off their chests. They should meet the next weekend and do it again. Same time, same spot. Letitia would need to return to B&Q for more supplies, while Melissa could make up any old excuse, as Matty wouldn't listen anyway. They said goodbye and Letitia sashayed between rows of cars that glistened like disco balls in the sunshine.

It only occurred to Melissa later that evening, staring at the bedroom ceiling while Matty snored, that Letitia had gone in a completely different direction to where she said that her van was parked.

* * *

The following Saturday morning, Melissa made her excuses and left Matty with the kids in front of Netflix while she drove out of town, bristling with an excitement she couldn't place.

As she entered the B&Q car park she was thrilled at how the centrifugal force from the curve of the access road tightened the seat belt against her chest. She enjoyed the way the speed bumps rattled her buttocks as she made her way alongside a grey gabion wall, passing a parked Vauxhall Corsa with its door wide open. A man in tracksuit bottoms sat with his legs outside the car, head hung down. He glanced up and momentarily caught her eye with a desperate look as she continued around the corner to the space she'd occupied the week before, near the dented shipping container.

After all that anticipation, the wait was interminable. Melissa switched on the radio to pass some time. A news reporter talked about the latest moor fires. People were fleeing towns and villages in the Peak District. They said it was the worst year for it yet, right across the northern hemisphere. California. Siberia. Greenland. All that permafrost melting and those long summer droughts. Global warming had gone past the tipping point, the reporter said. Melissa kept hearing this over and over, that the catastrophe was already under way. But at B&Q, everything looked the same as it always had.

It was the end of the world and she was totally bored.

The next news item was about eight deaths during riots at the migrant detention camps in Kent. Three of them children. With a sigh, she switched the radio off. There was too much bad news these days. It had become unbearable to listen to current affairs shows the way she used to. But whatever passed for popular music on the radio wasn't for her either. Instead, she sat in silence with her phone, grimacing at her friends' Facebook updates, hoping to find one from someone leading a duller existence than her own.

Rachel Hagerty, recently remarried, was off to Borneo and looking really fucking happy about it, obviously.

Melissa's cousin had just got an Open University degree in forensic psychology.

There was a photo of Alan and Fee Granger doing star jumps at the top of Ben Nevis.

A colleague from her company had announced she was leaving to focus on her inexplicably successful Etsy business, selling earrings made from bottle tops.

Worst of all, Julie Thompson had posted a picture of a sunrise with the words: 'Start by doing what's necessary; then do what's possible; and suddenly you are doing the impossible.'

Dear god.

Melissa craved a post where someone admitted they'd made a bad choice. That they'd wasted their time. Fallen off the rails. Like when the little-miss-perfect head girl from her schooldays admitted she was battling alcoholism. Or when that QAnon prick Alan Smedley posted an incoherent rant about how a paedophile network at the bank had stolen money from his account. These posts made her feel better about herself. It was awful, she knew it. Like she was a pitiless Facebook predator, hunting her newsfeed for weaklings to feast upon.

A sudden commotion disturbed her. A few feet away, a couple of crows fighting over some discarded fries were interrupted by a gaunt, bald man in a dirty anorak who looked a bit like Nosferatu. As the birds flapped away, he stopped to observe Melissa for a few moments, rocking slightly from side to side, chewing his lip. He stepped forward as if to approach, then changed his mind and sidled behind the shipping container.

Bloody weirdo.

She hit the internal door lock, glancing around her for the nearest security camera. Mind, even if there was a camera, who would be watching? Who would put a stop to anything terrible happening? She'd read all kinds of stories about people in superstore car parks getting stabbed or robbed. Cameras never seemed to make a difference. She doubted they were ever actually recording.

Melissa was grateful when Letitia emerged from between a Nissan Micra and a Ford Mondeo. She leapt down from the SUV, beaming and waving. Almost as soon as they'd hugged and said 'hi', Melissa felt the overwhelming urge to release all that pressure which had built up inside of her. She told Letitia about how glad she was to find someone she could talk to, truthfully, about how she really felt. And what she felt was tired.

Tired of Matty.

Tired of being a parent.

Tired of customer service management.

It had only been meant to give her some income after university while she sought a career in publishing. But then seven years drifted by, in which she got married and bought a house. At that point it seemed foolish to switch career and jeopardise their mortgage. Now she was forty-one years old, running her team online because the office had closed during the pandemic, never to reopen. Which meant endless days of working at home, communicating with invisible people by email. Endless evenings watching television with Matt while Axel sulked upstairs and her eleven-year-old daughter Macy stared at her phone like a zombie.

Was this how modern life was supposed to be? Or had she done something wrong? It felt like they were in prison, awaiting some heinous sentence for a crime they did not know they had committed.

Melissa became shamefully aware that she was the only one talking but Letitia was an eager listener. She gripped her arm tightly, as if to take her pulse, the numerous rings on her fingers digging into her flesh, throat pulsing with tiny swallowing motions, murmuring with enraptured empathy.

When it was over, Letitia breathed deeply. But instead of responding with words of wisdom, she pulled out a cigarette and lit it. The ensuing silence wasn't exactly awkward. Just strange. Melissa had thrown Letitia a ball, expecting her to play the game, but Letitia had simply pocketed it. She seemed distracted. Her nose twitched and she sniffed air, as if she had caught a scent. She tossed the cigarette butt into the woodchip mulch and grabbed Melissa's shoulder.

'That's it, girl,' she said, without her usual smile, those green eyes drilling into her. 'Until we meet again.'

Melissa desperately wanted to say something to make her stay, but she felt glued shut. Fixed to the spot, she watched in dismay as Letitia ambled towards the pine trees without looking back. Once she was out of sight, Melissa slumped against the car, feeling drained. Light-headed. A little bit sick.

There was a rustling behind her. A rat scurried towards one of the Rentokil traps poking from beneath the fronds of the box hedge. It stopped near the entrance hole, as if to consider its options.

'Don't,' said Melissa. 'Just don't.'

* * *

After the kids were in bed, Melissa stood at the back door while Matty watched *Match of the Day*, looking out over their Astroturf lawn, smoking a sneaky cigarette. She thought about her last trip to the car park. Letitia's farewell was so abrupt.

'Until next time,' she had said.

Did that imply they'd meet again at the same place, next Saturday?

Or was that just a big brush-off?

Melissa wished she had asked for an email address or phone number. She scoured Facebook looking for Letitias but none of the profiles matched. She googled 'Letitia decorator', but nothing.

That night, Matty asked her for sex, something they hadn't done in a long time. For the first few minutes, all she could think about was Letitia. Her kindly face, listening to her moans and groans, nodding fervently, tell me more, Melissa, tell me more about your problems. Give it to me. Give me the hard stuff.

Then it wasn't Letitia at all, but the B&Q store looming over her with its massive orange face and its dirty edges, those pine trees thrusting upwards, the Valspar paint-mixing machine hammering away and the sound of someone singing 'You can do it when you B&Q it.'

She begged Matty to stop.

No more. No more.

But it wasn't over. Later, she had a dream that she went to B&Q with Macy but once they were inside it looked more like a supermarket, not a DIY store. When they opened one of the upright freezers, there was a creepy man inside with dark holes instead of eyes, who handed them a box of fish fingers. Macy screamed but Melissa turned to her daughter and told her that it was okay. He lived there because he had nowhere else to go.

The next morning, she was still thinking about B&Q. Days turned into nights, into days, into nights, and the yearning to go there and talk to Letitia did not go away. And when Saturday came round again, she returned to the same spot, where Letitia's cigarette butts, stained with her lippy, lay on chippings that bore the faint imprint of their feet from the last encounter. She reversed into the slot and waited, scrolling through Instagram, occasionally looking out the window, hoping to see her. It was a long shot, but not an impossible one.

After a while, a Vauxhall Astra reversed into a space about four empty lots away. The sole occupant was a man around her age, wearing a beanie hat. Once parked, he didn't get out of his vehicle or switch off the engine. For over half an hour he sat there. It was disconcerting. She just wanted him to do something. Eat a sandwich. Make a phone call. Anything. His presence was unbearable.

Go away, you sad little man, she thought, *be gone with you.*

It was usually alright being parked out on the edge, with only her thoughts for company, but not when guys like him made it feel tawdry and desperate.

Melissa was about to give up and leave when she saw Letitia, cutting between two vans, carrying a new pot of paint. But she didn't approach Melissa's car. She didn't seem to see her at all. Instead, she walked towards the man in the stupid hat. Melissa slid down into her seat as far as she could, watching Letitia approach his passenger door. His window rolled open and she bent down so all Melissa could see was her buttocks waving from side to side. They talked for a while like that, but she couldn't hear what they were saying.

From this angle, Letitia looked disconcertingly like a sex worker propositioning a john, but she was not like that. It couldn't be that. But then, what was it?

Did they know each other? Had he been waiting for her all this time?

Was this a rendezvous?

Eventually, the man got out of the Astra and stood in front of Letitia. He was wearing ironed jeans and a denim shirt that was far too big. It was as if a wizard had shrunk him inside his clothes. Double denim. Never a good look. But on him it was a catastrophe. It looked like he had been crying but he was smiling now that Letitia was here. Well, she couldn't blame him for that.

The pair talked some more. This time Melissa could make out fragments. 'Ex-wife... depressed... we used to come here... bad memories... socket button screws... bedsit... wish they would come and visit... Bosch combi drill... discount sale.'

Letitia nodded as he spoke, just like she did when Melissa poured out her heart to her. She clutched the man's wrist in the same way with that same backward tilt of her head. Then she said something to him. It must have been significant because the man's Adam's apple bobbed up and down as he tried to swallow back his emotions.

What a baby. It was hard to imagine Letitia falling for this nonsense. But at the end of this excruciating exchange, Melissa was mortified to see them walk together through the car park in the direction of the store. The man paused once to activate the remote-control lock of his Astra, and then they were gone.

The air inside the SUV was stifling. Melissa jabbed at the button for the electric window. It opened with a buzz that sickened her. All this pointless convenience. All this hopeless luxury. All this wasted energy.

Enough.

She exited the car and began to walk away from it. She couldn't face driving home. Not right now. She needed air. A brisk circuit of the retail park would let her gather her thoughts and calm the fuck down. Perhaps on the way she might bump into Letitia. She could pretend she was heading into the store to buy more paint and that their encounter was a happy accident. *Oh hello*, they'd say to each other in unison, *do you come here often?* Or something like that. Then they'd guffaw at their little in-joke. HA HA HA HA HA HA HA. Letitia with her big laugh. Melissa slapping her own thighs, doubled over. Like the day they met. And after they recovered from their hysterics, Letitia would explain what she was doing with that ridiculous man in their sacred spot on the edge of the car park and everything would be okay.

The clouds sat heavy and low. An occasional drop of rain bloodied the dry tarmac as she traversed the cracked lines of parking bays, tracking the box hedge as far as it would go. She passed a woman in an expensive Mercedes, slowly applying red lipstick while a mournful love ballad blared from the stereo; a Volvo with tinted windows, its solitary occupant a shadow within; a Ford Fiesta, parked at an angle, the driver with his forehead on the steering wheel, face obscured. She tarried a few moments, observing him closely, concerned that he was dead, until he reached out his left arm, clenched his fist, and began to strike the dashboard repeatedly.

Okay then.

Eventually she reached a thick mass of cotoneaster, bursting with berries. There was a crude break where people had repeatedly forced their way through, the trail littered with disintegrated McDonald's packaging. Probably those late-night car cruisers who left figure-of-eight marks on the tarmac, stomping to their makeshift racetrack with drinks and burgers.

Melissa felt compelled to step into the gap. As she did so, a whiff of cotoneaster flashed her back to a moment in time. She and her mates at the Tesco near their school, sneaking into the maze of hedgerows with a spliff during a lunch break. She remembered bursting into hysterics at the sight of discarded underpants covered in shit and how they found women's stilettoes in a little clearing – 'right scary' they said, puffing on the joint, coming up with elaborate theories about the murderer who left them there. Funny, she hadn't thought about that incident in decades. She'd pushed it to the back of her mind as a childish misdemeanour, best forgotten. But now it felt like the happiest time ever.

At the other side of the hedge, a grassy slope led to a lower car park for the other major stores in the retail park: M&S, Currys and Halfords, as well as a Costa Coffee and a McDonald's Drive Thru, its golden arches glowing like a neon church.

This car park was smarter. Cleaner white lines, less litter and fewer people lingering. Red walkways for pedestrians were lined with shrubs in giant pots and ornate cast-iron litter bins. There was a smell of hot dogs. In contrast to the drab corrugated grey and orange of B&Q, the modern glass-and-steel edifice of Marks and Spencer reflected a shimmering vision of the car park back onto itself. It was like staring into a parallel dimension. She strained to catch herself in the reflection but she was too far away to register in the seething mass of metal machines; nothing more than a footnote in the story of cars.

As she made her way along the pavement, a besuited man gave Melissa a suspicious stare. When she looked down, her jeans were dirty. There were a couple of tiny leaves in the creases at the knee. He must have thought she was one of those saddos lurking at the edges of car parks.

How embarrassing.

Melissa hurried on until she came to a little wooden bridge, surprising amidst all the concrete and asphalt. She stopped in the middle and leaned against the barrier. A few metres beneath was a narrow gully filled with shingle and lined with blocks of old, worn stone. In the lower car park it was only a shallow trough running between the trolley bays, but once it passed under the bridge it became a deep gorge that cut through the elevated B&Q car park. Steep banks on either side were littered with dead needles from the pine trees she'd observed from her parked car these past few Saturdays.

How curious. It looked like a dried-up stream, or perhaps a trackway from a time before the retail park existed. It was remarkable that despite all her visits over the years, she had never noticed it. Then again, why would she?

There was a slope leading to the track at the side of the bridge with a muddy trail gouged into it. Perhaps formed by the same nocturnal denizens of the car park who created the gap in the cotoneaster. Melissa was tempted to follow it. She could walk up the path and see what was at the end. Maybe an interesting historical feature. Sure, it was a little foolhardy. A lone woman in a concealed alley beneath B&Q. But it was unlikely that anybody uncouth would be there in the daylight. Besides, she enjoyed the shiver of trepidation. It took her back to those Tesco truancy days. That time when life was still wide open and even smoking a poorly rolled joint in a stinking hedgerow could be an adventure. If this was teenage life, with all its restrictions, she marvelled at what thrills adult life had to offer. In the forbidden edges of the local car park, she had once dared to dream.

Nervously, Melissa entered the gorge, feet crunching on stones. She noticed there were circular iron hatches along the sides of the channel. They looked old. Victorian perhaps. The light was already gloomy because of the amassing black clouds and the canopy of bushy pines above her, but there was a thickening of the darkness as the vale narrowed. She stopped and checked for an escape route. It would be easy to scramble up the bank in a few seconds, she figured. While she couldn't see it, the car park was still there. She could hear a man barking at his kids. An engine turning. A baby crying. These sounds drifted into the gully and settled like mist. Offered her some comfort.

This was silly, a woman of her age, doing dares with herself for the hell of it, but she continued onwards, wondering how the path could feel so much longer to walk than it appeared from the outside.

Soon there was another noise. But this time it was from up ahead, around a slight bend. A voice. Quiet and whiny, almost mewing, but certainly human. Melissa slowed to a more cautious pace, readying herself to make a dash for it.

A few steps more, and she could see that the route terminated in a circular area, walled with mossy stone. Yellow water seeped from the cracks and dripped a glutinous beat on the concrete floor. In the centre was a bench and a bin for cigarette ash.

There were three people there. One of them was the creepy bald man in the anorak who she had spotted earlier by the shipping container. One of them she couldn't see properly, because he was lying on his back.

The other was Letitia.

She and the bald anorak man were on their knees, on opposite sides of the prostrate figure, bowed as if in prayer, faces close to his chest. For a moment, it seemed like they might be giving him CPR. Or that they were already weeping over his demise.

With rising panic, Melissa ran forwards. 'Letitia! Is he okay? What happened?'

Letitia stood up quickly, pivoting to face her – startled, like a kid caught smoking. Now Melissa could see that the man on the ground was wearing double denim and a beanie hat. It was the sad little guy from the Astra. His eyes were closed but he murmured a feverish, whimpering babble.

'They don't respect me... they don't... I never see them any more... it's not fair... all the lies... I never... all lies... they don't come to see me... I'm building them a bunk bed...' He started to choke up. A horrible strangling noise like a distressed cat. The bald anorak man grinned, nodding his head up and down to the rhythmic undulations of the sound.

'Is he alright, Letitia?'

'My, my, aren't you the curious one?' said Letitia, frowning. 'I have to say, I didn't expect to see you here. You must be in far worse shape than I thought, girl.'

'I wasn't... looking... for – I was – I was just having a wander. But really, is he alright?'

'Does he look alright?'

'No.'

'That's your answer then.'

Letitia sounded odd. Rather cold. A bit aggressive. Then again, what did Melisa really know about her? Aside from that opening gambit at the paint counter and her inspiring story about ditching her career, she had not revealed much more than was necessary to start a conversation. She had made a simple cut in the flesh and then waited for Melissa to bleed out.

It was always Melissa talking while Letitia listened. She was a good listener. Always listening.

'Shall I call an ambulance?' Melissa reached for her phone.

'No, he's not that kind of ill,' said Letitia. 'Nothing a hospital's gonna fix, anyway. Tell you what, sit down here with me. Let's talk about it.'

'I don't think…'

'Come.' Letitia gripped her wrist and drew her to the bench as if she was a naughty child. It didn't feel right to complain about her life, what with the distressed man lying there on the ground like that, and that weirdo in the anorak hunched over him, doing nothing to help. But one look into Letitia's eyes and Melissa numbly acquiesced, feeling faint suddenly. She noticed there were a lot of sealed tins of paint and orange B&Q bags around the bench, like discarded props.

'I missed you at the car park earlier,' said Melissa woozily. 'I thought – I hoped – we were meeting again but then… you were with him…'

The double denim man was muttering something about divorce settlements while the anorak man uttered little grunts and sighs of appreciation. Neither of them seemed to notice Melissa's presence at all.

'…I didn't know if you saw me or if you wanted to see me,' said Melissa. 'But then I came to look for you. Sorry.

God. I don't mean to sound weird. It's not like that. You know. Not weird. I'm not weird. It's just…' Her words began to slur. She felt a heaviness in her bones. Prickling skin and shivers. Like she was coming down with the flu. 'It was just that I needed to talk. I really needed to talk… to you… to anyone, really… anyone… I hate it at home… I hate me… and I don't know why but I…'

'Yeah, it's okay, tell me all about it,' said Letitia, cradling Melissa's scalp gently, easing her back onto the bench. 'You must be very tired.'

'I am, I am.'

'So tired.'

'Yes…'

'You say what you need to say, Melissa. Don't hold back.' Letitia leaned over her, lips parting to bare brilliant white teeth. 'Let it all out.'

* * *

It was dusk when Melissa clambered up the bank of the gorge and stood for a while by one of the pines, looking over the fence into the car park where a fine rain sparkled in the glare of the floodlights and oily puddles welled in the tarmac. Her head was thick. Mouth dry. She had no idea how long she had been down there or what had happened to her. Her left hand felt unusual. It took her a few moments to realise that her wedding ring was gone.

Oh well. It didn't matter. She would find another ring. There were always more rings. More fingers. More hands. More people. So many people coming from miles around to congregate in this car park. They wanted to buy home improvement goods but what they really needed was a banishing ritual to release them from their burden, like those liberated young car cruisers who scorched black rings into the tarmac at night to keep their demons at bay.

She could see them now, the weary remnants of B&Q's congregation, leaving the infernal church. A woman in a hijab pushed a pallet trolley towards a Perspex bay, while her husband loaded their purchases into the boot. A man in overalls approached his white van. A young couple ducked into a smart car, headlamps flashing as their vehicle swung out from its space.

These people were too strong and healthy for her. But at the furthest edge of the car park were those who sat alone in silence, staring out the window or gazing at their smartphones, scrolling through social media feeds in an interminable hunt for consolation, desperate for help which they never believed would come, and so – unable to think of an alternative – remained in limbo. Even in the dimness of the evening, she could tell which cars they were because a greenish aura emanated from them. Domes of loneliness shimmering on the perimeter. A scent, too, like rotten meat, carried on the breeze to her lair in the trees. It made her hungry, but not in a way she recognised. A heart hunger. A hole in the chest that must be filled.

Eventually, it became impossible to resist. Melissa clambered over the fence and made her way to the perimeter, where a Skoda was parked, throbbing with phosphorescent light.

Inside was the silhouette of an elderly man.

Melissa was fully aware that she looked a bit of a state. Pine needles and cotoneaster leaves were stuck to her clothes. Hair damp from the mizzle. But she knew that the old man would wind down his window when she knocked upon it three times. He would find it surprising when she said, 'I'm sorry for bothering you, but are you okay?' A little odd, perhaps. Yet at the same time, he would feel relief that somebody had asked him, and an overwhelming desire to reply.

He would speak. She would listen. And when heavier raindrops began to drum on his roof, he would invite her inside the car to talk some more.

THE SLIME FACTORY

The promotional video came out of the blue. A real surprise. Nobody had seen Roman Nesterov in public for almost five years. The eccentric billionaire had shut himself away inside his research complex, leaving his spokespeople to deal with nervous shareholders and enquiring journalists. No interviews. No social media updates. No statements. Total blackout. He could have died, for all we knew. Now here he was on my phone screen, standing in front of the Organistrive logo in a black suit and top hat, looking extraordinarily tubby. His once-chiselled features had become grotesquely bloated, and either he had gone totally bald or he had shaved his head. But it was Nesterov alright.

'I have a vision of a future,' he announced to camera in his sonorous Slavic tones, eyes twinkling inside their fatty pits, 'unshackled from our bondage to fossil fuels. Where organic computers run our lives without electricity and transportation is self-sustaining, self-repairing and even self-navigating.'

The lilting melody of 'The Lark Ascending' struck up as the film cut to a panoramic view of hills dotted with sheep beneath a blue sky. Victorian railway bridges arched across wooded vales. Church spires poked above thatched roofs. Fields of corn and barley were crisscrossed with flowering hedgerows. Ducks and geese paddled on a lake as swallows swooped over the rushes.

This footage was surprising because it didn't seem to be CGI, but a real landscape, presumably Nesterov's private estate in the Cotswolds. If so, it was either a digitally enhanced film or a physically manipulated landscape, for it was a far cry from the Britain I knew: the charred moorlands; the polluted rivers; the barren mountains; the drowned cities and filthy air. It looked like the Gloucestershire of the 1940s, not the 2040s.

'This is the place to which we truly belong,' Nesterov intoned, 'and to where we can return, after the fires and flood, the death and disease, and all else we have suffered. Our future lies in the past of our dreams, but we need dream no more.'

As the camera panned across the bucolic vista, the carriages of an extremely long locomotive could be seen vanishing into a tunnel.

'In a special event on Friday the 11th of July, I shall unveil a radical new technology that will save humanity by transforming it. A special invited press audience shall bear witness to our society's rebirth. I do hope you'll join us for the live stream.'

The film ended with a still of people in summer dresses and suits, crowding a traditional branch line railway platform, waving handkerchiefs and craning their heads for an approaching train. The tagline read: *Organistrive: A Better Time Will Come.*

'Fuck,' I said to nobody in particular, the bedsit being dismally empty, as always. Just me on an unmade bed, with dirty coffee mugs and a bunch of flickering laptop screens. I had been awaiting this moment for so long, it took a few minutes to register what I'd just seen. After years of silence, Nesterov was about to open the gates of his slime factory to the media. This was the big one. I absolutely had to be there for the press conference. Not only to write a story about the flamboyant tycoon, but to help Nia find out what he had done to her missing boyfriend.

Nia and I met at university, where I was a visiting lecturer in digital media, and she was studying for a PhD in bioscience. At a house party we bonded over tequila slammers and a shared interest in environmental activism. I'd written about the attacks on the cryptocurrency systems, the airport sieges and port blockades as battles in a class war against the inequalities of climate change impact. The only way for humanity to survive the emergency was to unite against the gang of super-rich industrialists who caused most of the problems yet were the most insulated against the ecosystem's collapse.

That might be true, agreed Nia, but for her the solution lay way beyond the class struggle. She believed in a Marxist solidarity with non-humans, from rocks and trees to insects and fungi. For too long we had treated humanity and nature as separate entities. In fact, she said, sprinkling salt onto her fist, we should stop seeing things as *other* altogether. She picked up a slice of lemon with her slender fingers. It was the othering of things that was the problem. Human beings were not separate. Not really. The human body was a legion of microbial organisms. The human mind was a series of interconnected operating systems. The human world was but one among many. The world of chalk. The world of tin cans. The world of dust mites. She pushed a shot glass towards me. The world of tequila. Salt, drink, lemon. All these objects were conscious at some level.

Nia licked the salt, knocked back the shot and bit on the lemon, without a flicker of discomfort. If we were to survive ecological annihilation, she told me, human beings had to give up the illusion of stewardship over the Earth and instead forge a symbiotic union with other species, even other substances.

Bang. That was it. Instant crush. I could not resist her militant ontology, raven hair and tolerance of hard booze. We immediately started going out, although we never moved in together. In hindsight, it was not the most romantically involved affair. Nia disappeared into her work for weeks on end, barely responding to my messages. When she emerged, she wanted to eat, drink and screw like there was no tomorrow – and I was more than happy to oblige. Three or four days would pass in a blur, then she'd be gone, as if recharged by hedonism, and she wouldn't give me another thought until the next time she rang my doorbell, both actually and metaphorically.

The subject of Nia's research was the slime mould *physarum polycephalum*, which I knew only as a gooey yellow entity that lived on forest floors. A weird fusion of fungus, plant and animal, it seeks food by snaking out tendrils in all directions. Those which fail to find nourishment shrink away while others establish a perfect network for delivering nutrients. They were the perfect organisms for helping humans design infrastructure systems. Researchers placed oats on city locations on a map of Japan and watched the hungry slime forge the most efficient railway network. They tried the same with British motorways, revealing flaws in the routes of the M4 and M74. Later, NASA created an algorithm based on slime mould to map the cosmic web of dark matter distributed across the universe.

But slime mould's most exciting quality was the way it retained the knowledge of its previous successes and errors in its protoplasmic veins. When slime moulds merged, they transferred this knowledge and used it to improve their navigational abilities. The bigger they got, the cleverer they became. This capacity for problem solving and memory storage had applications in the creation of organic computer chips, which was what Nesterov's company began to develop in the 2020s.

Organistrive had already developed a means of storing large amounts of data as DNA sequences inside plants. 'The complete works of literature of mankind can be contained within a tree,' boasted Nesterov. 'Soon we shall live in Edenic gardens of knowledge.' Now they wanted to develop fully organic operating systems. To do this, they used genetically modified slime mould to create 'Memresistors', controlled by light and chemicals, rather than by wires and transistors. Organistrive's systems began with basic functions like operating alarms, security gates and prosthetic limbs. Then Nesterov embarked on more ambitious projects involving communication, transportation and artificial intelligence.

In 2037, he announced the world's first living computer. It made a worldwide splash on the news. He was all over tech and culture websites, photographed in his trademark retro English gentleman fashions, with headlines like SLIME KING, BREAKING THE MOULD and GROW YOUR OWN. He was even *Time* magazine's Person of the Year. Then, without warning, the eccentric billionaire shut himself inside his research complex, dubbed *Willy Wonka's Slime Factory* by the press, and vanished from public view. His public relations team would only say that he was working on something big, and he needed to focus all his attention on it, away from the limelight.

There was never any doubt in Nia's mind that she would join Organistrive as soon as she completed her doctorate. Her Kenyan heritage not only barred her from most other career avenues and higher level university posts, it also put her in constant danger of internment or deportation. Nesterov had many faults, but racism wasn't one of them. All he cared about was employing the world's best brains. And while Nia was no capitalist, she agreed in principle with what Nesterov was trying to do. A collaboration between humans and slime mould was one way we could transcend the ecological catastrophe. When the oil ran out and old systems failed, our knowledge could ooze through the protoplasmic tubes of new organic networks. Civilisation could endure in harmony with the biosphere. She believed this was what Nesterov wanted, deep down, despite his showbiz bluster. He declared with typical bombast that his biological technology could help humans survive 'the biggest climate disaster since the Younger Dryas asteroid impact of thirteen thousand years ago', and there was the sliver of a chance that he was right. With our options rapidly running out, it was a straw worth clutching.

When Organistrive hired Nia without even an interview, it was the end for us, romantically speaking. She had a destiny in biological engineering. Mine was in journalism, or whatever that constituted these days. I was pleased for Nia, but I knew I was unlikely to see much of her again once she entered Nesterov's private estate. The sprawling grounds included not only his factory, but villages for employees, family and friends, connected by a local railway network, among acres of countryside, fenced off from the public and guarded by a garrison of security troops. With enough wealth, it was possible to continue a twentieth-century lifestyle amidst the disaster of the twenty-first century. You just needed to establish a territory, pay off the government, and protect your land with walls and weapons. There was no protest from the public because they didn't really know what was going on. The media were in the service of the government, and the government was in the service of oligarchs like Nesterov.

The only silver lining to this dire situation was that it allowed me to eke out a living as an independent journalist. I worked anonymously for underground websites, funded by an uneasy coalition of anti-fascist organisations, environmental activists, former media barons and wealthy donors shocked by the obliteration of a free press. We sought every chance we could to poke a hole in the canopy of oppression and let in some light of truth. The mass executions at migrant concentration camps. The hit squads who stole people from their homes at night. The radiation leaks from the subaquatic concrete tomb that contained Dungeness nuclear power plant. The cover-up of an outbreak of sentient bacteria on the icebreaker *Salvo* which drove its crew insane. These should have been major media stories but they existed only on dark web news sites in pieces by the likes of me, written anonymously out of fear that one night they would come hammering on my door, too.

Unlike Nia, I had never been convinced by Nesterov and his biological experiments. I didn't trust his obscene wealth. His power. His unaccountability. But there had been no way to write a story about him. Despite numerous offers of life-changing money for a scoop, I couldn't get close enough to anyone who worked for him, past or present. The only outsiders ever permitted into his estate were government cronies and hacks from state newspapers. I knew that Nia was my only way in, but I didn't want to abuse our relationship or jeopardise her career. I set up an encrypted message system for her to get in touch if she ever wanted to tell me anything, or even to say hello, but she never used it. That was, until two years ago, when I was surprised to receive this message from her:

I need your help.

In the exchange that followed, Nia told me she was still a relatively low-level researcher in the company, developing bacterial colonies to run genetic programs in computers that used DNA molecules instead of wires. It was important work but she was disappointed that the major slime mould project, for which Nesterov had retreated from the world, was hidden from her. Staff were expected to work on their component parts without ever being informed about the ultimate goal. The rumour was that Nesterov's top scientists were building something extraordinary inside the gigantic hangar near the railway terminal of Rodos village, but there was no way to see inside.

None of this especially worried Nia until she embarked on a relationship with Thomas Riese, the recently divorced head of development at Organistrive. He was a charming, intelligent man, but she quickly realised something was troubling him. He cried out in his sleep. He would begin sentences that trailed off, as if he was desperate to tell her something. Often, he alluded to goings-on in the hangar, which he said were stretching the boundaries of what was acceptable. He complained that he was expected to make the most unreasonable sacrifice. On one occasion, she found him in the bathroom, weeping, a razor blade clutched to his wrist.

When Nia mentioned her worries about Thomas to one of the counsellors, they agreed to look into it. A day later, Riese vanished. She searched for him but her access card could take her only so far. There were rooms, corridors and chambers completely closed off to her.

I need to know if he has left the estate, she messaged me, *can you try and track him down? I am so worried.*

It was easy, at first, to research Thomas Riese. Born in London in 2001, he was a third generation German Jew whose grandfather escaped death in a concentration camp at the age of two and emigrated to Britain. There were plenty of articles about Riese's rise to the top of Organistrive, with pictures of him at conferences with Nesterov and tabloid newspaper photos of his wedding in 2030. The most recent was in a *New Scientist* profile.

However, as I began to dig deeper, I noticed something strange. There was no trace of his social media accounts. Many references to him had been redacted. I would click on links to find websites that were no longer recognised. After a few days, even the images I'd found on my initial search had started to disappear. He was vanishing from cyberspace right in front of my eyes. I'd never seen anything like it. It was hard enough to remove something permanently from the internet, never mind on this scale. And why such a focus on images of his face?

Nia thought it could only be Nesterov's doing. Nobody else would have that kind of power. *Something is going on,* she wrote, *something terrible. They say there are things living in the hangar. Big things. Villagers hear them howl at night. A lot of people feel afraid. Yet nobody knows why. Or at least, nobody that's left.*

The situation was becoming tense. Workers were frogmarched by security from the labs or their homes. Their phones would go dead. Intranet accounts closed. Social media accounts gone. Homes boarded up. That was the price of being suspected of sharing secrets with the outside world. The thing is, I never found trace of any of these leaks. No rumours on the dark web. We were none the wiser about the inner workings of the biotech giant. And it wasn't only the lower-ranking workers, either. Edward Silverman, Head of Research, completely disappeared. Most shockingly, Gordon Tanaka, the Chief Operating Officer, was sacked out of the blue and nobody had seen him since.

If they know I'm leaking this to you, wrote Nia, *I could be next.*

I looked for information on Silverman and Tanaka but my searches brought up meagre results. Like Thomas Riese, they were being wiped from the internet. Nesterov was disappearing people like some biotech Stalin, not only physically, but digitally. The only way I could help Nia was to get through the gates of Organistrive but there was nothing I could do about that. Nesterov's estate was 'in England' only in a topographical sense. Politically, socially, economically – even morally – it was another country. I had no way of entering without being shot on sight. That was, until Nesterov's surprise announcement that he was flinging open the gates of his slime factory.

It was only moments after I finished watching the film that I received this message from Nia.

I have your Golden Ticket. Please come.

And just like that, I was in.

* * *

The train pulled out from Paddington and headed west. As we passed Wormwood Scrubs, I could make out the slimy tops of tower blocks in the distance, poking above the water in what would have been White City and Hammersmith only ten years ago. Once the flood began it happened quickly. From Stratford to Battersea to Chiswick, whole tracts of London on either side of the Thames slipped beneath the waves. The city was the epicentre of a disaster but many of its denizens still clung to the water's edge, gazing out over their lost pasts – the barnacled flyovers, multistorey car park islands and subaquatic roundabouts – still believing the land would rise again.

Out towards the M25, smoke curled from industrial estates into a yellow sky as gulls circled the sewerage pits of shanty towns on the city's edges. We continued at a crawl through the overcrowded suburbs, where I looked down into back gardens with electricity generators, water butts and dirty kids, who prowled the sidings, throwing stones at us. After Slough the train accelerated through a countryside of waterlogged ditches, ramshackle pig farms and polytunnel networks. It was a depressing journey but things looked the same in whichever direction you left the capital. The English landscape was like a series of collapsed studio sets from a half-remembered twentieth-century film, its backdrops tattered, props in shattered piles, mouldering in pools of dirty water.

We arrived in Gloucester, where I joined a small crowd gathering on a platform for one of Nesterov's private local trains. I recognised a few famous faces from the government-allied news organisations. Nesterov had banned cameras, but these preening ghouls were still accompanied by assistants and makeup artists who could help conceal the shit smeared round their mouths from their constant arse-licking. I kept a low profile in case any of them twigged that I was one of those leftist renegade journos they liked to warn the public about, determined to bring down the state, or what was left of it. But as always, they were only interested in themselves and nobody paid attention as I sat by a window near the rear of the train, avoiding the stare of the trooper who stood guard by the doors, clutching a machine gun.

The final stage of my journey couldn't have been in starker contrast to what had come before. Verdant hedges, fields of wheat and wildflower meadows. Windmills and churches. Sandstone terraced houses with slate roofs. Thatched cottages. Tea shops and public houses. Old stone bridges from which couples in Barbour jackets waved as we passed. The vision of England portrayed in Organistrive's video had been realised through extensive replanting, rewilding, rebuilding and re-sculpturing. It was as if I was travelling through a giant diorama, like one of those landscapes built for a train set in a middle-aged man's attic. It was missing only the frozen plastic figurines and the giant human face of the operator rising above their artificial world like a sentient sun. Of course, Roman Nesterov was the top-hatted man-god who controlled this English fantasy.

We pulled into our final destination, the old-fashioned provincial railway station which had featured in the promotional video. All steep gables, baroque eaves, ornate ironwork and touches of Victorian gothic. As far as I could tell, this was a new station, built within the last decade, but the brickwork had been deliberately weathered. The whole place sepia-stained to look like the inside of a teapot. While some of the passengers gawped at its features in wonder, I refused its sick nostalgia. Nesterov was a vulgar magician who used simple tricks to line his pockets. They didn't work on me.

A man with a whistle ushered us off the train and we queued for almost an hour at the turnstiles as we were patted down by security, our phones placed in plastic bags and non-disclosure forms thrust in our faces. I couldn't see the point of a product launch in which nobody could take photos, report live, or even say what they'd seen. This wasn't really a press conference at all. We had been invited not to report, but to act as props in Nesterov's dramatic performance. I tried to hide my fury, not at Nesterov but these so-called journalists. I had never seen a more compliant herd of fascist enablers and authoritarian apologists. Fortunately, the security guard didn't find the mini smartphone recorder I'd wedged expertly between my buttocks. They should have known better than to mess with a pro.

Once released, we were directed through a subway beneath the station and out to the rear car park, where a large crowd of Organistrive's employees, friends and family were gathered in their Sunday best, drinking gin and tonic out of teacups. We were enclosed on three sides by stalls selling drinks, cakes and party balloons. A troupe of Morris dancers jigged to a minimalist drumbeat, surrounded by white-gowned maidens wearing garlands of flowers. In front of the crowd was an isolated railway platform built onto the car park, set up like a stage, with a cinema screen at the back and steps on either side, hung with colourful bunting. Two cherry pickers carried cameramen high above, one pointing his lens down at the assembled mass, the other at the stage where a small band of musicians was setting up. I couldn't recognise all the instruments. Aside from a drum kit and double bass, there was a battered honky-tonk piano and an organ made from steam whistles, the kind you might get in an American travelling fair.

The scene was reminiscent of one of those corporate family afternoon events with face painting for the kids and a tombola, had it not been for what was looming behind the stage: the hangar Nia had told me about, a windowless façade of brick and steel with three giant double doors – all closed. Train tracks ran out from beneath each of the doors, all the way to the stage, where they converged in parallel lines alongside it. I wondered if I could slip away and get a closer look, but despite all the festive gaiety the car park was surrounded by security guards, brandishing weapons.

My heart sank. To get to the hangar, I would have to break through this protective ring, pass around the stage, and then run over two hundred metres of train line to reach the building, where there were more armed men standing by the main doors. The best I could do was find Nia. I moved slowly through the body of people, searching for the Kenyan girl I once knew. Eventually, I saw her standing near a cupcake stall, wearing a long black coat. Her hair was almost entirely grey. Face drawn. Back stooped. It had been, what, ten years since I'd seen her? I don't know why I'd thought she'd look the same. A decade working in a lab for a billionaire despot. All that agony over her missing lover. So much disappointment in her career. She looked older than her thirty-five years. Who knows, maybe I did too? I had dispensed with mirrors long ago and can't remember the last time I saw a photo of myself. It was only my carefully protected anonymity which allowed me to infiltrate events like this weird corporate fete.

Nia pretended not to notice me as I approached. Like me, she was aware of the camera on the cherry picker above, and who knew what eyes and ears Nesterov had on the ground? However, she clenched my hand when I brushed past and I stopped beside her, facing the opposite direction, pretending to study the various flavours of cupcake while I said in a low voice, 'You look good.'

'Liar.'

'Well hello to you too.'

Nia didn't smile. Her eyes remained fixed on the distant hangar, dark against the green hills beyond it.

'I wish we could talk somewhere,' I said. 'What's been going on?'

'Nothing and everything.' Nia grimaced. 'I don't know.'

'Tell me what I can do.'

'Just watch – watch what happens next. Then tell the story. The real one.'

'But I need to find a way to get close to—'

'Shhh – they're starting.'

A harassed-looking Organistrive official trotted up the steps to the stage and began speaking to the band, gesturing to where a white limousine with monster-truck wheels approached. With a 'one – two – three', the band struck up a jaunty instrumental that sounded like circus music and ragtime mixed with music hall. The limo doors opened and out stepped Organistrive's Chief Marketing Officer, followed by Helen Allan, the Secretary of State, and then by Roman Nesterov, in the same black suit he'd worn in the video. He looked even fatter in real life, his face almost a sphere, with ruddy cheeks, his eyes reduced to pinholes. He donned his top hat and puffed up the steps, giving a wave to the crowd, who clapped and whooped, waving embroidered handkerchiefs in the air, just like on the promotional video.

Without warning, Nia pushed through the crowd, working her way to the front, until I couldn't see her at all. I clicked the audio record button on the device concealed in my pocket, waited for a few moments, then made my own way through the throng, partly in hope of getting a better view, partly to stay close to Nia and make sure she wasn't about to do something stupid.

As I closed in on the first few rows, I spotted Nia at the front, about five people across from me. She glared at the stage, where the dignitaries took their seats beneath the screen as Nesterov ambled to the front of the stage and unhooked the microphone like a rock star.

'Thank you for coming.'

Applause.

'Long time no see.'

Laughter.

'As you can see, I've been eating on your behalf.'

More laughter.

'But of course, none of it matters, because we are all going to die and everything you care about will be gone.'

Grim silence.

'Every endeavour in human history. Totally meaningless. Forgotten. That is what will happen after this great extinction, if it continues unabated and we don't change. But who is to blame for our predicament? You, for trying to eat and heat your home? The industrialists, for offering these things to you? No, I'll show you how we got here.'

Nesterov waved a pudgy hand at the screen, where a CGI film showed giant sloths, mammoths and woolly rhinos moving through leafy undergrowth. Humans crouched among them, turning meat over a fire, eating handfuls of berries and mushrooms.

'This world was once our Eden,' said Nesterov. 'But during the Neolithic era, a great crime was committed against nature and, by default, against humanity itself.'

The film cut to Stonehenge in the sun, priests in cloaks bowing, legions of men and women carrying baskets of bread along ceremonial corridors of white chalk.

'In liberating ourselves from hunting and gathering, we rebelled against not God, but against the idea of ourselves in nature,' Nesterov said. 'We became separated. We didn't know it at the time, but it was an act of war.'

Now the film showed a golden field with medieval farmers threshing corn, windmills turning in the background and folk dancers dressed in white gowns.

'For a time we enjoyed our dominion, but then came industrialisation.'

The scene changed to a landscape of mills and factories, chimneys belching smoke, and earth churned up by diggers. This was quickly overlaid with shots of power stations and pylons, motorways, shopping centres and aeroplanes. Flames licked the bottom of the film, steadily consuming the screen until it was all fire.

'The global warming disaster cannot be undone,' Nesterov said. 'More cities will sink. More lands will burn. We are paying for the original sin of the Neolithic. The enslavement of nature for our ends. The pillaging of resources. The destruction of habitats that were really our habitats too. But I want to end that war. Today, in view of this congregation of friends, family, workers and invited press, I propose a new way forward. A fusion of species that might allow us to go back to the beginning. Back to Eden. But with all our astonishing art, science and knowledge intact. A lasting legacy for the future.'

The screen lit up again with the bucolic English scene from the promotional video, showing a train crossing a railway viaduct in a wooded vale.

'I have been working on the development of organic machines that can think, navigate and repair themselves, allowing us to travel and communicate even if power supplies fail.'

In the distance, there was a metallic squeak as one of the hangar doors began to grind open. Nesterov turned and pointed at it. 'Behold! The world's first living locomotive!'

The band struck up once more with their insane rockney barrelhouse oompah, as what at first appeared to be an early twentieth-century train engine, with a smokestack and pistons, eased out of the darkness and began to approach the stage, where Nesterov beckoned it towards him like you might entice a shy horse.

Once it was in the sunlight, I could see this was no ordinary train. There was no steam. No sign of electrical input. No mechanical noise that could be heard over the music. The engine itself wasn't shiny and metallic, but wet and fleshy. The skin visibly writhed with muscular movement, and I could make out intricate arterial networks pulsing with yellow slime. Along the locomotive's length, tendrils hung down like millipede legs, gripping bony coupling rods and using them to turn the wheels. There was something even weirder about the circular smokebox door at the front of the engine. But it was only as it got closer that the realisation hit me. It was a face, stretched across the entire disc, made of veiny blue skin, taut and translucent. The big eyes swung from side to side, scanning the crowd.

A wave of nausea came over me. Others could see it too. There were gasps. Cries. A scream. The sound of someone being sick.

'This is not artificial intelligence,' Nesterov declared, over the clatter and parp of the music, 'but actual intelligence. The consciousness of slime moulds, plants and fungi, united with the knowledge of human beings.'

I looked across at Nia, whose countenance in that moment haunts me to this day – an expression of unabated horror, as if she was gazing upon the visage of death itself. I could see her body shake violently as the train groaned to a halt behind the stage, emitting an exhausted sigh, now in full view of the astonished crowd. Tears pooled in its eyes as tiny spores floated upward from fruiting blobs on its roof. There was an overwhelming smell, like honey-marinated meat left in the sun. I could see now that there was no driver. No mechanical parts and no fuel. The creature was a mass of sinew, bone, slime and skin. There was something uncanny about the face, too. Something I couldn't put my finger on until I heard Nia scream, 'Thomas! Thomas!'

As she uttered those words, I swear the rubbery, lipless mouth opened and contorted as if it was trying to reply to her.

'That's Thomas Riese! Thomas Riese!'

Nia flung herself towards the stage, but before she could get even a few metres, two guards tackled her to the ground. An anguished bellow came from deep within the train, like a terrified cow in an abattoir. Instinctively, I tried to move towards Nia, to help her, but the crowd surged to see what was going on, trapping me in the crush. She was dragged to her feet and hauled away to the sound of circus music, screaming 'Thomas!' over and over again. Before I knew it, they'd taken her beyond the stalls and out of sight.

'Apologies, ladies and gentlemen,' Nesterov laughed nervously, his cheeks flushed, 'there's always one, isn't there? Thomas indeed! Good name for a train, though!' The honky-tonk piano trilled in response, 'Dah-dah-dah-dah dah-dah daaaaaahhhhhhhhhhhh.'

I looked around at the crowd. Implausibly, they had quickly composed themselves after the fracas. Most were beaming up at the abomination on the platform. Some still waved hankies in the air. Clearly, Nesterov was insane, and a terribly insane thing was occurring right in front of us, but at the same time, it also didn't feel that way. Not in the reality of the moment, with all the gin in teacups, balloons and Morris dancers, and folk in nice clothes watching intently, instead of running screaming in all directions. Within minutes the horror had been normalised.

'And there's more, ladies and gentlemen,' Nesterov bellowed, clapping his fat hands together as the remaining hangar doors opened simultaneously and two more monstrosities emerged, blinking in the sunshine. Their train engine forms were similar but with idiosyncratic differences in length, colour and bulk. Different animals grown from similar moulds. It was only as they drew closer to the stage that I recognised their hideous visages, for I had studied both faces intently during my search for information and – unless Nia and I had been gripped by the same pareidolic delusion – I could see obvious resemblances to Edward Silverman and Gordon Tanaka.

The two new arrivals lined up in parallel, mournfully lowing at each other, films of greasy fluid spilling down their sides and dripping from their undercarriages. As the crowd burst into excited chatter, fixated on the spectacle, I took my opportunity to force my way back through the crowd until I could escape through a gap in the stalls. I ran full pelt across the car park towards a row of faux-Georgian houses, where the two guards were grappling with Nia beside an armoured security van parked on a cobbled street.

'Stop! Leave her alone!' I pulled out my secret phone and held it aloft. 'I'm streaming this live,' I lied, 'and you're now on camera. Stay where you are.'

The guards stopped and regarded me for a moment, with smirks on their faces. Nia, slumped between them, cried, 'Look out!'

I didn't know what she meant until a few seconds later when I felt something thud into me. There was a lot of pain very suddenly, then everything went black.

* * *

You could say I was lucky. They didn't do much damage, the men who knocked me out. They smashed my phone, of course. Obliterated it. Didn't even give back the shattered pieces. But for whatever reason, I was not considered a threat and they put me on a normal train with some soldiers who escorted me in silence to Gloucester, where I was unceremoniously hurled onto the platform.

Back in London, I got straight on the internet to see how the world had reacted to the bizarre events of the afternoon. All I found was a very slick film of the event, edited and manipulated to remove Nia, and me, and the people who screamed or puked at the sight of Nesterov's diabolical creations. This must have been what they streamed 'live' but with delay enough to tweak and embellish. They had digitally touched up and smoothed out the trains to remove the more visceral details.

There was plenty of outrage on social media, of course – the kind of nugatory chatter which the state gladly permitted – but all the government-sponsored news sites declared the launch a triumph. A damned good show. A tonic for the nation.

The fuckers.

I tried to contact Nia on our encrypted channel but there was no reply. I couldn't think where else to look online. Nia didn't have much of an internet footprint. She'd never bothered with social media and her entire career had played out within the Organistrive world. Now she may as well not have existed.

Opinion pieces came out over the following week with speculation about what self-growing, self-driving, self-navigating transportation might look like if rolled out. They admitted these prototypes were not perfect yet, and might not come into service for perhaps five years. That seemed to quell some fears but Nesterov was concerned enough about the reaction to launch a propaganda campaign. This consisted of a family-friendly series of films about anthropomorphic, driverless trains, set in the landscape of Nesterov's mutated Gloucestershire. These were sanitised toytown versions of the monstrosities I'd seen in the flesh. Thomas, Gordon and Henry looked much more like traditional locomotives, their faces infantilised, with that damned circus ragtime playing over the opening credits.

It was appalling to watch, knowing the grim truth these films represented. But I had to keep checking the latest episodes, looking for clues about what Nesterov might be up to behind the scenes. It was the only thing I could think to do. The doors to his slime factory had closed once more and he'd stepped up the military guard on his estate. After my exposure at the conference, they'd have my face and fingerprints logged on their systems for sure. One glimpse of me on their security scanners and I was a dead man – a disappeared man – or something even worse.

I put feelers out to see if any of my comrade journalists were up for an investigation. They said they'd see what they could do. I didn't hold my breath. Instead, I stayed at home and drank gallons of cheap wine, reading old novels written in those eras before I was born, when people believed there was a future worth living in.

A year later a new character was introduced to Organistrive's propaganda film series, in an episode entitled 'Thomas's Silly Mistake'. She was a tank engine from Kenya, and I was horrified to recognise her face.

ACKNOWLEDGEMENTS

Thanks to everyone who has published my fiction over the years...

Gary Budden, Kit Caless, Dan Coxon, Ashley Stokes, Robin Jones, John Lavin, Marian Womack, Richard Brook, Luca Csepely-Knorr and Jared Shurin.

Thanks also to Jen Orpin for inspiring 'My Father, The Motorway Bridge', and to Vince Haig for the cover.

'We Are the Disease' was first published in *The Shadow Booth Vol II*, ed. Dan Coxon (2018)

'When Nature Calls' was first published in *Unthology 10*, ed. Ashley Stokes and Robin Jones (Unthank, 2018)

'A Dream Life of Hackney Marshes' was first published in *Acquired for Development By...* Ed. Kit Caless and Gary Budden (Influx Press, 2012)

'Thenar Space' was first published in *The Lonely Crowd* Issue 9, ed. John Lavin, (2018)

'Tyrannosaurs Bask in the Warmth of the Asteroid' was first published in *An Invite to Eternity*, ed. Gary Budden and Marian Womack, (Calque Press, 2019)

'The Levels' was first published as 'The Knucker' in *This Dreaming Isle*, ed. Dan Coxon (Unsung Stories, 2018)

'My Father, The Motorway Bridge' appeared in *You Love Me Really: Journeys Through Landscapes of Post-War Infrastructure*, ed. Richard Brook and Luca Csepely-Knorr (2021)

'Meet on the Edge' was first published in *Out of the Darkness*, ed. Dan Coxon (Unsung Stories, 2021)

ABOUT THE AUTHOR

Author photo: Sara-Louise Bowrey

Gareth E. Rees is a writer of fiction and non-fiction, based in Hastings, East Sussex. He's the founder of the website, Unofficial Britain (www.unofficialbritain.com) and the author of *Unofficial Britain* (Elliott & Thompson, 2020) *Car Park Life* (Influx Press, 2019), *The Stone Tide* (Influx Press, 2018) and *Marshland* (Influx Press, 2013). He has also contributed short stories to numerous anthologies of weird fiction and horror.

Influx Press is an independent publisher based in London, committed to publishing innovative and challenging literature from across the UK and beyond.

Lifetime supporters: Bob West and Barbara Richards

www.influxpress.com
@Influxpress